FREE

Edited by Dorothy Davies

FREEDOM

GRAVESTONE PRESS

CONTENTS

R.I.P.

Arlen Feldman

The casket was relatively high-end. It was cobalt blue, made of thick eighteen-gauge steel, with silver handles and hardware. The interior was lined with light blue velvet, with matching pillow and throw.

Thanks to an incorrectly installed seal it was not, however, waterproof.

Barely two days after it had been buried, water from the incessant rain had wormed its way through the seals, carrying with it the biologic pathogen currently wreaking havoc on the surface.

The pathogen found itself in contact with organic material and started to attach itself and reactivate the deteriorating cellular machinery it encountered. Nerves and muscles were not exactly restored, but were jury-rigged into a simulation of their original function. After this was done, the pathogen started to flood the brain stem with nutrients.

Six days after Jerry Weber died of a massive coronary, his body began to move.

More accurately, it could be said that the body started to twitch. There was no objective and no drive. Had it been an isolated case--and had anyone been able to see into the pitch-black casket--it might have been miraculous.

Had one of the survivors on the surface seen it, they would have had a different reaction--

identifying Jerry Weber as being a *Stage-One Twitcher*. What was left of the medical research community would have known that this phase would last for somewhere between three and nine hours, depending on the condition of the affected corpse.

For a corpse, Jerry Weber was in fairly good shape. He was reasonably fresh and, for religious reasons, had not been embalmed. The twitches lasted for about four hours while the pathogen diligently went to work hijacking Jerry's amygdala.

The pathogen could survive for a long time by consuming what it considered to be non-critical parts of Jerry--but it could survive considerably longer by having him consume external nutrients. To get Jerry to assist in providing said nutrients, it installed in its host an insatiable hunger.

In theory, any nutrients would do, but the pathogen was far from perfect. Ideally, it "wanted" its host to avoid consuming already-infected food sources. The way that it did that had the side effect of only targeting humans.

This stage had been dubbed "the hunger" by those above who had managed to survive long enough to get around to naming things.

Jerry stopped twitching and, infused with a desperate need to feed, made every effort to do so.

Unfortunately for him, he was buried in the dark, five feet underground, in a damp steel box.

The combined instincts of Jerry and the pathogen joined forces to drive him towards the surface and food. Fists, elbows, knees, feet, head, all pounded against the top of the casket--the sounds muffled, even in the confined space, by the velvet lining. At first, the amount of force in Jerry's atrophied muscles was pitiful, but the pathogen started strengthening the muscles, using energy freed from the demolition of now unnecessary organs, such as the gall bladder and the skin.

If Jerry had been more religious, he would have only been wrapped in a shroud, or, at most, a wooden casket with no nails and hinges. It is *just* possible that he would have been able to escape from either of those. He would still have had to make it through the earth to the surface, but it might--maybe--have been achievable.

But the 4,800 pounds of dirt sitting on top of the casket's cobalt-blue top made it impossible for the lid to be raised. The solid steel meant that it was impossible to break through.

Nonetheless, Jerry spent the next sixty hours trying to do exactly that.

In truth, because of their age and their inaccessibility, very few of the pathogen-powered monsters roaming the surface came from cemeteries. Morgues and hospitals were the primary source. Then accident victims, as panic started to spread. Then victims of the victims.

Aside from the sounds of his own attempts to escape, Jerry's world was quiet. The surface was currently a very noisy place.

***

After a while, even the soft thuds against the velvet faded out. Jerry was now a S*tage-Two*

9

Twitcher. This phase was deceptive--as the doctor who coined the phrase learned to his cost. Given the opportunity, a Stage-Two Twitcher would become active very, *very* quickly, if presented with an appropriate stimulus.

But at this point, the pathogen was saving its energy. Or rather, it was saving Jerry's energy. Without further nutrients, the host could last for several weeks in this state, although towards the end of that period, there would not be enough left of the host to move.

Two things happened in Jerry's favor at this point--if favor is the right term to use.

First, lacking a better place, people started dumping corpses in the graveyard, hoping perhaps that someone would eventually get around to burying them. Many of these corpses had been infected with the pathogen, but had subsequently been shut down via the expedient of chopping through the brain stem--or, as often worked, implanting a bullet, at speed, in same.

Second, it continued to rain.

The rain carried nutrients to Jerry--not much, but enough to be useful. It also brought new and different versions of the pathogen--versions that had experienced the bright world and had had the chance to evolve just a little bit.

Small parts of Jerry's cerebrum had previously been activated. Enough of the occipital lobe was working to provide at least basic visual processing, although this was entirely useless in the pitch-black casket. Corners of the parietal lobe had been needed in order to coordinate movement. But now the newly improved pathogen started flooding nutrients into the frontal lobe.

This was a risky trade-off. The frontal lobe could solve problems--such as how to escape from a box buried under five feet of dirt. On the other hand, the frontal lobe was huge and therefore expensive in terms of resources. Worse, it relied on the temporal lobe buried underneath it--another huge, expensive lump of fatty gray matter--the chunk that handled memory. Without memory there is no ability to reason.

On the surface, this technique had driven the pathogen's victims to conquer such complex tasks as opening doors, climbing ladders and, in one extreme case, using a hammer--literally already in hand--to pull down a barricade.

Jerry's major accomplishment with his extra, though still extremely limited brainpower, was to rip away the casket's lining before attacking it once more with fists and feet. It was no more effective, but it was much louder.

In the outer world, the intensity of the rain had increased, which did not do much for the mood of the already miserable survivors. It should have, though, since the rain interfered with the primitive senses of the infected--making the huddled and hiding people a tiny bit safer.

The popularity of dumping bodies in the cemetery had also increased and had even been given something of an official imprimatur by the placement of a printed sign reading "Emergency Body Storage Sight." The misspelling of *site* had not slowed anyone down.

The material at the bottom of the casket was now completely saturated with liquid and nutrient-filled water was starting to pool. This created a sort of equilibrium--*just* enough nutrients were getting to Jerry to keep the pathogen active and able to continue expending resources.

Whether the success of pulling down the casket-lining spurred it on, or whether it had no other strategies, the pathogen fed more of the new nutrients into the frontal lobe, simulating dopamine for the neurons that were operational enough to be stimulated by it.

A groan passed Jerry's lips. Considering that his larynx was bone dry and flaky and that there was no mechanism for pumping air through the vocal cords, this was actually quite impressive--the release of a last puff of breath. No one was there to hear the sound, but it sounded just a bit like the word "Laura." Given that Jerry had a daughter named Laura, this might not have been a coincidence.

There were no further sounds from Jerry, although his lips did continue to move.

***

It started with a swirling of colors in front of his eyes, resolving into disjointed memories. Words associated themselves with the colors. Sky. Ocean. Grass. They all faded to black.

More words came. Hot. Cold. Damp. These connected together into more complex ideas. *I* am cold. *I* am damp. *I* am. *I*.

12

Jerry felt very strange. He had no idea where he was but, despite a slight chill, he felt relatively comfortable.

He had memories of a great deal of pain in his arm and in his chest. He remembered his teenage daughter screaming.

And then... nothing.

Maybe he'd had a heart attack? It would not have been the first. If so, was he in a hospital? But it was so dark. Even in the middle of the night, hospitals had some lights and blinking machines.

One thing he knew for sure--he was really, really hungry.

In hospitals there were usually buttons to call the nurse. He reached out to see if he could find one. His hand ran into the side of something and something similar on the other side. And something right above.

Possibilities crowded into Jerry's brain, but he quickly pushed them aside. It was ridiculous to even consider such a thing. It was the twenty-first century after all. People didn't get buri...

No, ridiculous.

He tried to take a deep breath, but couldn't. How sick was he? It didn't feel like he was breathing at all.

If he couldn't detect his own breathing, maybe a doctor couldn't, either. Maybe they had thought he was dead?

"Oh, God," he thought. "The bastards buried me alive!"

Now fear and anger possessed him and he started pounding on the casket much like he had

13

earlier. He also used his feet to try and push out the bottom of the casket, then flipped himself over and used his back against the lid, to no avail. He tried to stick his fingers through the seam between the base and the lid and actually managed to touch damp earth, losing most of his fingernails in the attempt, but getting no closer to escape.

These were exactly the sort of strategies that the pathogen would have been trying to stimulate and, if it had had any sort of awareness, it would have been pleased with the results so far, ineffective as they were.

The hunger was really getting to Jerry now. He needed to eat. It was odd, though. It wasn't steak in his mind, or his wife's brisket. He was thinking about food, but the images in his head were of blood and throats and raw, steaming guts. He simultaneously wanted to drool and to throw up, though he no longer had the ability to do either.

An image of Laura popped into his head, unbidden. His beautiful daughter, crying as the ambulance men loaded him onto a gurney. For just a second, he pictured her throat, torn and bleeding. The picture came with a flash of hunger. He shuddered, forcing the image from his mind.

And now he was just angry. How could they have possibly done this to him? He pounded his fists against the casket lid, hearing the crunch of a finger bone splintering, but feeling no pain.

The more rational part of Jerry's returning mind eventually managed to assert itself. He abruptly stopped striking out and dropped back onto the silk lining. He needed to think.

***

It is easy to fall into the error of assigning purpose to the pathogen. It was not showing any more intelligence than, say, the vibrio cholerae bacteria that attacked the lining of the large intestine, that simultaneously made its victims miserable and spread cholera to a wider audience.

The pathogen was not worried or angry or panicking. It was just following the biological laundry list encoded in its genes. When a particular strategy failed to produce the expected nutrient/enzyme intake, a secondary strategy kicked off.

So, the pathogen had no ideas at all and certainly no idea that it had gone too far with Jerry-- that the parts of Jerry responsible for cognition were becoming active and that those parts of the mind that managed memory and had not rotted too far, were now slowly coming back on line.

The freshest memories were of a great pain in the chest and arm, his teenage daughter Laura screaming and then a vision of a dark tunnel as the retina was starved of oxygen.

This set of memories was too painful to examine and Jerry pushed them away. He could do that because his sense of self was slowly returning. The pathogen-induced hunger was still strong, but the frontal lobe had a lot of experience in overriding the body's immediate need to feed.

He tried to concentrate, to plan, but even at his best, he would not have been able to come up with

15

any solutions to his current dilemma. Only outside help could save him and he had no way to contact anyone.

Carefully, as if probing a missing tooth, Jerry thought about his daughter--wondering where she was. He had no idea of the chaos currently sweeping the surface, but if he had, he would have been comforted by the fact that Laura was barricaded in a shopping mall with a group of other survivors. Jerry had not been a big watcher of movies.

A picture of his wife suddenly popped into Jerry's head. This was possible because more of his temporal lobe was active now, but Jerry just felt a wash of guilt that he hadn't thought of her before. Edith was a strong woman, and stubborn. If she knew he was down here, she'd move heaven and hell to get him out. But she didn't know.

Jerry was now lying almost fully-immersed in a pool of contaminated nutrients. This didn't help with the hunger, which was insatiable, but it provided some more opportunities to the pathogen.

When alive, Jerry had been one of the many people who believed in the myth that people only used ten percent of their brains. That would have been a very poor evolutionary choice, considering how expensive brains were to operate, using more than a quarter of the body's energy.

In reality, most people--even politicians--used almost all of their brain, although not all of it at the same time. Generally, a person might use twenty to thirty percent at any given moment. This was irrelevant to the pathogen, which started activating more and more of Jerry's brain, firing up virtually all of the pieces that were still intact, and providing all sorts of additional makeshift connections.

The amount of heat generated by this process was considerable, but fortunately, Jerry's head was now sitting in a pool of gooey rain water, which did a great job of keeping him cool.

Again, it is foolish to assign intent to a pathogen, but the serendipitous results achieved by this mélange of coincidence would have been almost exactly what the pathogen would have wanted--if it wanted things.

Jerry's understanding grew in leaps and bounds. Despite having no interest or understanding of biology, he began to grasp his situation and needs, becoming more rational and less emotional as he considered his options, limited as they were.

And then things started to get weird.

Until this moment, Jerry had assumed that he had been buried alive. Now, however, he realized that this was not the case. Jerry now knew, *knew* precisely what was happening to him, how the pathogen worked and what the obvious result of this would be to his species.

It is unclear whether he was tapping into some sort of Jungian Collective Unconscious, whether he now had some supernatural access to the minds on the surface, or whether his brain had stored all of those Discovery-channel shows his wife had insisted on watching. Possibly it was some combination of all three.

No matter which, Jerry, who in life couldn't make a sandwich without instructions, was suddenly confident that, given an appropriate laboratory, he could not only create a cure for the pathogen, but also make use of its unique abilities to cure half the diseases that also plagued mankind. The sensation of crystal clarity brought Jerry a powerful joy that he had never experienced in life.

Unfortunately, Jerry was still stuck in a soggy box more than five feet underground.

What he needed to do was to make some sort of tool. In life, Jerry had been an accountant. It is possible to think of careers that would have provided *less* suitable experience for his current situation, but not by much. An accountant *might* have been buried with his calculator and pen, which wouldn't have been great tools, but better than nothing. His wife, however, had not thought to do so, burying him only with a photo of his family which, while nice, was not useful.

However, Jerry *had* been buried with his shoes. This normally would not have been helpful either, except that many of Jerry's customers worked on construction sites and Jerry had been terrified of tetanus. For this reason, almost all of his shoes, even his fanciest dress shoes, were steel-toed.

The casket was roomy enough for Jerry to be able to reach and take off his shoes, confirming that they were, indeed his steel-toed dress shoes. In his current state, this was neither surprising nor a relief--it was simply how things had to be.

The tip slid into the defective seal before starting to compress the leather, but using his hand as a hammer, the steel plate, acting as a wedge, opened a small gap.

Jerry twisted the shoe, expanding the gap to a width of a few inches. Not enough to escape, but enough to stick his arm through if he didn't mind losing some skin. And some muscle. And a bit of bone. Jerry didn't mind.

Very carefully, Jerry started pulling in earth from the side and then from the top of the casket. Because the earth was damp, it didn't immediately fall, but left a cavity. As the pressure slowly eased on the lid, he was able to use the other shoe as a shovel to reach even further.

It took a long time. He had plenty of time to spare. It wasn't as if he was going to run out of air. Had it been at all sentient, the pathogen would have been cheering in excitement--its strategy had worked.

The pathogen contained awareness, it was not worried about Jerry's revelations and plans. Honestly, even those who knew and loved Jerry the best, had they known of his ideas, would have given them little credence--even assuming they could have got past the whole being-dead thing.

Less than twenty hours after he'd removed his shoe, Jerry had made the gap wide enough for his body to slip through, albeit by sustaining damage that would have severely incapacitated a living person. Now, instead of being inside a steel box, he was buried in wet earth.

Jerry stood up.

Actually, it was a somewhat more gloopy process than that, but basically just that simple. The casket was buried the standard five-feet below the ground. Jerry was six feet tall. With a sucking sound, his head and a bit of his shoulders popped out of the ground. It took a while for him to free his arms, but once he did, he started digging himself out. This was a lot of work, but did not take long.

In the past, the amount of effort he had just exerted would have had Jerry gasping in pain. Now, though, other than being hungry, he actually felt wonderful. He couldn't remember feeling healthier. Had a doctor examined him, the doctor would *not* have agreed.

Quite apart from apparently being dead, Jerry was quite literally falling apart due to days of necrosis, followed by the ravages of the pathogen as it fed on the bits of Jerry that it didn't consider to be important--not to mention the damage he'd done to himself while escaping his theoretically last resting place. If there had been a mirror around, Jerry would have run screaming from his own reflection.

This would go a long way in explaining what happened next.

Although it was still raining, Jerry's head was no longer sitting in a pool of cooling water. He still *knew* what he had to do, but the crystal clarity was fading. He realized that he had a very short time to act. The odds of him finding a lab were minimal and he couldn't talk.   He needed to leave a note.

He found the "Emergency Body Storage Sight" sign and ripped it off of its post. It was printed paper in a plastic cover. Jerry struggled with this for a bit. His coordination was failing as his brain heated up. The pathogen was not responsive enough to realize that, having achieved a major part of its goal, it would be a good idea to ease up.

Now that he had paper, Jerry needed something to write with. As he'd already checked, he knew that he didn't have his own pen, but it was possible that he might find one in the pocket of one of the many corpses lying around. He spent many minutes searching without luck. The world was getting hazier now and Jerry was fighting to focus.

He found a small stick and, lacking anything better, dipped it into his own chest. The blood had mostly coagulated, but the cocktail of pathogen-laced fluid was a brownish-gray color that he hoped would dry visible.

Using the back of one of the corpses as a writing surface, Jerry started laboriously to write. His brain's temperature had shot up and not even the pathogen could help him concentrate.

Seth Kovak had come with his friend Josh to deliver another truck load of corpses and had exited the truck to open the gate. He spotted Jerry and had no doubt of his status, vis-à-vis being alive. Two weeks ago, he would have missed the shot, but Seth had recently had a lot of target practice.

Hollow point ammunition is considered "safer" because it is less likely to exit the target and hit something else. It is not, however, safer for the target. The bullet hit Jerry's head and entered his brain, turning into the classic mushroom shape that simultaneously keeps the bullet contained and does a lot of additional damage. The bullet bounced around several times, eviscerating whatever it had missed the first time through.

Since the bullet was supersonic, there is no need to ask whether Jerry heard it coming. He was dead before the sound reached him. Well, more dead. More classically dead.

"What the fuck was he doing?" Ernie asked. He had seen the shot from the cab of the truck and had got out to see the results.

Seth shrugged, then walked over to Jerry's body and kicked it over. He picked up the sign.

"Looks like it was writing a note," he said, handing the paper to Ernie.

Ernie squinted at it, trying to make out the--it must be said--terrible handwriting.

"I think it says *Laura*."

"Who the fuck is Laura?" said Seth.

Ernie shook his head. "Fucking zombies," he said, then, pulling out his own gun, he shot Jerry three more times.

Ernie's gun shot full-metal-jacket ammo rather than hollow points. Most of the shots went through Jerry without stopping and buried themselves a few inches into the ground. A few went deeper, finding fissures and cavities in the moist earth. One lucky round went right through Jerry, deep through empty pockets in the soaked ground and straight through the wooden lid of Marsha Kendleson's casket, buried two days after Jerry.

Although made of wood, the casket had, until that point, done a good job of protecting its occupant. Now, a sample of the pathogen that had, until then, only existed in Jerry, was transferred to Marsha--but hardly enough to matter. Infected water, though, started dripping in through the new

22

hole in the lid of her casket. The pathogen went to work immediately.

The Warden

Joseph J Dowling

Somewhere, a tap dripped. Calloway couldn't sleep and, judging by the soft, moist slapping sound coming from the other bunk bed, he wasn't alone. He sighed and chewed his lip, waiting for the inevitable grunt as Jones climaxed and the creak of sagging bedsprings as he rolled onto his side, panting slightly in the humid cell air.

Jones's rhythmic heavy breathing soon intensified into a familiar, buzz-saw snore, leaving Calloway to stare, red-eyed, at the cracked ceiling, dotted with spreading patches of black mould, almost invisible against the flaking gun-metal grey. But he knew they were there; he knew every inch of sad, crumbling cement above.

By the time the cold hue of early morning filtered through the miniscule, barred window which offered his only evidence of an outside world, Calloway had long since given up on sleep. As soon as the light allowed it, he picked up his book of chess puzzles and returned to one which had troubled him for days. He knew the solution required a knight sacrifice to smash open black's defences, but he couldn't deduce how to contain the opposing king and deliver checkmate.

The buzzer sounded for breakfast, shattering his fragile concentration. He sighed, launched the book onto the scarred flagstone floor and descended the rickety ladder.

"Game for faggots," sniggered his bunk-mate Skelly, without provocation.

Calloway laughed and said, "Funny, coming from such a moron as you. Why not try giving that tiny mind of yours more exercise than your fat fucking mouth for a change?"

Skelly sat up on his bunk and glared at Calloway, but soon broke eye contact. He hawked, shifting something substantial inside his deviated nasal cavity and spat a streak of green mucus toward the slop bucket, where it hit the side and crawled slowly down the pale aluminium.

In his guttural east-end drawl, Skelly muttered something incoherent under his breath. Calloway stared hard at Skelly and considered putting him in his place once and for all, but McKay was due to arrive imminently.

The cell door lurched open, revealing a weathered, deadpan face. McKay, the solitary guard they'd encountered since arriving at Wormville Borstal, stooped and wordlessly shoved a tray of paste-like grey porridge and boiled eggs towards them before slamming the door shut.

The rest of the morning passed without incident until, bored and still frustrated from the earlier exchange, Skelly paced the room. The others attempted to ignore him. Porter, the youngest of the four, huddled further into his pillow, making sure not to catch anyone's eye. Finally, Skelly stopped, put his hands on his hips and glowered at him.

"What you lookin' at, queer?" Porter blinked rapidly and scrunched up his eyes, refusing to meet his chief tormentor's withering stare. When Skelly asked again, he could not ignore the question.

"I... I ain't," he stuttered.

"Ain't what? A goddamn queer?"

"I ain't," Porter repeated. Skelly turned away, apparently satisfied and Porter exhaled a relieved breath, unaware that Skelly had his fists balled tightly. Suddenly, the boy charged and mounted him. Porter tried to protect his face with his thin and worn pillow, but Skelly ripped it away. His sneering face was inches from the younger boy's, with the lingering stench of the morning's eggs on his rancid breath.

"Say it. Say you're queer!" Skelly spat, covering Porter's face with spittle.

"I ain't, I ain't," Porter screamed, while a flash of skinny wrists lashed his reddening cheeks with open-handed slaps.

"Yes, you are. I know what little bitches like you want and I'll give it to you." Skelly jumped up and pulled his stiff prick from his stained pyjama bottoms. Porter flailed at it and looked desperately around the room for help, but Jones lay facing the wall, ignoring the confrontation, while Calloway leaned back with his arms behind his head, observing.

"Suck it, cunt!" Porter stopped struggling and stared at the quivering member in front of his face. Skelly yanked his hair painfully and forced his lips towards it. A slight aroma of soured milk reached his nostrils and he screwed his eyes shut. Porter

26

began to cry and gag, choking as the other boy gripped his head and frantically thrust towards release.

Hundreds of prior insults, beatings and humiliations danced in front of Porter's eyes. Everything turned red and orange as Skelly bucked and grunted. When a thick jet of bitter semen rocketed into the roof of his mouth, Porter clamped his teeth down and locked his jaw. The iron taste of blood filled his mouth. After a second of stunned silence, Skelly sank to his knees, shrieking in unabated agony, blood oozing through his fingers as he clutched his groin. Porter spat out the chewy gristle of his severed member.

"Holy Christ!" said Jones. "He's bit off Skelly's dick! Fuck this, I'm gettin' McKay." He rolled off his bed, flew over to the thick iron door and banged with both fists. "Guv, guv, you'd better come, bloody quick!"

The prostrate boy's high-pitched whimpers were drowned out as McKay's thundering footsteps grew close. With a stiff *clank*, McKay unbolted the cell door and stormed inside.

"What the fuck's goin' on 'ere, then? Someone's getting…" He stopped mid-sentence as his eyes fell upon the stricken Skelly, who'd turned the soft grey colour of a lizard's belly. He looked up at Porter's half-open, red-smeared mouth. A single wiry eyebrow rose questioningly at an acute angle and he reached for his baton. "What've you gone and done, boy?"

Porter stopped moaning and instead began to thrash and wail as McKay lunged forward with his stick raised. Jones watched, flinching with every vicious blow—each punctuated by a scream—until he couldn't watch anymore. But Calloway's attention never wavered as he flexed his enormous fists. McKay only grew more enraged as Porter slipped into unconsciousness and continued the barrage with renewed enthusiasm.

"He's had enough," cried Calloway, at last leaping to his feet. McKay's arm paused mid-swing and he turned.

"You wanna go see the Warden, son?" His truncheon arced again, but Calloway easily blocked the blow with his right forearm, locking the guard's elbow. With his left fist, he hooked McKay savagely in the ribs, knocking the wind from him. Calloway pushed his captor over and quickly straddled him, pinning his shoulders to the unforgiving floor.

With both hands now free to inflict damage, he rained down heavy, accurate blows. Jones joined the fray, unleashing a roar of pent-up aggression as he launched a boot at McKay's defenceless skull, shattering his temple. Almost simultaneously, Calloway's crushing final strike landed in the spongy mass of McKay's eye-socket as it caved in. Calloway stopped and slowly pulled himself upright. Neither boy could tear their gaze from the shuddering man's pulped face.

"Oh, we're fucked now," said Jones, breaking the silence. "You gone an' killed him."

"*Me?* You're the one who booted the cunt's head in. Swings and roundabouts, 'cause we're both buggered." He turned to Porter, who'd regained consciousness and sat cross-legged, rocking softly and groaning. "He attacked us, right? You saw it?" But Porter couldn't summon a reply and instead stared at Skelly as he slowly bled out.

"Fuck him, he's gone soft." Calloway bent over the motionless screw, plucked a weighty set of keys from his waistband and held them aloft. "Let's get out of this dump."

"What about Skelly?"

"Skelly's beyond help. He might be alright if it clots, but we can't do nothing for him."

"And what about the other guards?"

"What other guards? You ever realise we've been here months and seen nobody except McKay? Never even met this fucking Warden character."

"Do we leave 'im, too?" Jones jerked his thumb at Porter.

"Fuck him, if he can't get it together." Jones shrugged and the pair moved towards the door. But, as Calloway struggled with the stiff lock, Porter released a despairing cry.

"Don't leave me here with them. Please!" He jumped up, skidding on the vast, growing pool of Skelly's blood.

The three boys stepped out into the corridor. To the right, they discovered an immediate dead end, while the other direction stretched out for a hundred yards and bent around a corner. On each side were cell doors identical to their own and a decrepit shower room. They stopped and flicked open the hatches of several rooms—all were empty—and the only one which showed any signs of life was McKay's office. It was unlocked, so they entered.

"See if you can find a lamp or McKay's torch," Calloway said. The room was mostly bare, with a neat stack of paperwork on the unremarkable desk which had no other furniture except a hard, uncomfortable looking wooden chair for company. On the ledge of a barred window, offering a view of nothing but another brick wall and a sliver of grey sky, a chunky old wireless radio piped out classical music, almost inaudible against an ever-present background hum. Clouds of choking dust rose from everything they touched.

"Nowt 'ere worth taking," Jones said. After searching for a few more minutes, they gave up and returned to the corridor, following its continuous gentle curve until they discovered a large wrought-iron door blocking their path. Calloway rifled through the keys until he found one which fitted. It took all his dexterity to turn. The latch opened with a metallic squeal and the door groaned a few inches ajar. He pulled it wide enough to reveal a narrow staircase.

Jones hesitated. "You sure we wanna go *down*?"

You see any other goddamn doors? I just want out, don't care how," barked Calloway. Jones shrugged and inched his way down the dark stairwell, followed by the other two boys. Calloway counted the stairs and reached a hundred before losing interest. Still, they moved further underground.

"How deep does this shithole go?" But Jones found his question rendered redundant as they rounded a bend, which straightened out into a lengthy arched passageway. As they walked, an occasional naked bulb bathed them in a pale glow, interspersed with lingering shadows. Freezing droplets of water leached through the curved brickwork above and dripped onto their heads.

"What the bloody 'ell was that?" Jones said, pausing as a long, ripping belch echoed through the tunnel.

"Probably the pipe work down here. Must be ancient," said Calloway, sounding unconvinced. They slowed to a crawl as they approached two rusted brown doors, opposite but slightly offset from each other.

"Try these, eh?" said Jones and Calloway scoffed dismissively. Some of the keys fitted, but none would turn the ancient locks. After he'd tried every key on the ring twice, he admitted defeat.

"No good."

"Give 'em here," Jones said gruffly and reached to snatch the keys. Calloway rose to his full height and eyeballed the boy, who stood a good three inches shorter.

"I said, it ain't opening. Do I look like a complete mug?"

"Alright, keep yer 'air on." Jones shrugged and began walking in the only available direction. Porter followed close behind, but Calloway stood rigid, noticing a sudden cold gust of wind which sent a shiver through him. He caught up with the other two boys as they rounded a right-angled bend.

"There's a breeze coming from somewhere. If air's getting in, perhaps we can get out."

"I really 'ope so," said Jones. The floor sloped gradually downwards and a growing quantity of water seeped from above, until tiny rivulets formed at their feet. An occasional rat flashed past.

"Fuck, looks like another dead end up ahead," Jones said.

"Can't be," Porter gasped, clawing at his chest and hyperventilating. "I… I can't breathe."

"Stop whining and calm down, Porter. If there ain't no exit, how did we get inside…?" Jones's voice trailed off with the realisation he had no recollection of ever entering the facility. He knew he'd suffered a life of some sort, but he couldn't grasp memories of anything before Wormville Borstal. They all groaned as they reached the bare brick of another solid wall. Jones spotted something and doubled back.

"Look, there's a hatch," he said, stomping on a corrugated metal surface and sending waves of hollow reverberation through the tunnel. "Try the keys."

Calloway dropped to his haunches and examined the keyhole, which appeared much wider than the others. He selected the largest key on the ring and eased the huge hunk of brass into the lock, which turned smoothly. He located two recessed handles, pulled the hatch open with barely a squeak and propped it up on a metal rod. Calloway peered into the pitch-black chamber below and muttered to himself in frustration as he realised McKay probably carried his torch on him.

"Jones, you smoke, right?"

"Funny time to start, ain't it?"

"Don't be smart, lad. Need a fucking match to see what's down *there*," Calloway said, stabbing a finger into the darkness below. "Otherwise we gotta go back and get McKay's torch off his cunting corpse."

"Just playin' wiv ya. Damn, you're uptight," Jones said, pulling a matchbook from his pocket and handing it to Calloway, who ripped it from his fingers and struck a match. The narrow space amplified the sound as it lit, sending a tendril of sulphur-scented smoke into the stale air. He launched the match into the void, followed by another as the first hit running water and fizzled out.

"Only twenty-odd feet down. Gotta be some kind of sewer system."

"After you," Jones said, flicking his head at the ladder which led into the darkness. Calloway glared at him but said nothing and began his descent. "Ladies first," Jones added, inviting Porter to clamber down next. Calloway landed with a thud, causing a furious squeaking as a seething mass of rats scurried away.

"Ugh," Porter howled, "I hate bloody rats."

"Yeah and I'm sure the fuckers 'ate you even worse."

"Shh!" Calloway lifted a finger to his lips. It was the same noise as before—a huge burping groan—but louder this time. Calloway lit another match. It illuminated their dirty, sweat-slicked faces, but little else except for another arch-rimmed tunnel, far narrower and more worn than the last. Under their feet, two inches of greenish water flowed ever deeper into the Borstal's unseen bowels, but it appeared they could travel in either direction.

"Which way?"

"Let's try uphill for once." Calloway turned and began marching, Jones following close behind. The taller boy's hair scraped the ragged brickwork above and he cowered slightly. Porter scampered to join them, but his foot slipped into a hole and sunk into something soft. He pulled it out with a sucking sound, took another step and cried out.

"My shoe! Wait, my shoe got stuck. I gotta find it!" Jones and Calloway stopped and looked back. Porter was hopping on one foot, trying to avoid soaking his exposed sock any further. The two boys groaned in unison and resumed their march onwards, leaving him blindly searching for his shoe in the sandy surface below.

As their eyes adjusted to the gloom, further detail became apparent—enough to suggest it really was an old sewer system.

"Hey, I bet we can find another ladder like the last one and it'll take us to the surface, probably on a road towards town." But *what* town Jones could not recall.

"Perhaps, but it'll have to be a seriously long ladder. We must be an easy hundred feet underground by now."

"How can you be sure?"

"I counted most of the steps. Aldwych tube station has a-hundred-and-sixty steps and we must've done more than that. The Piccadilly Line is a hell of a lot deeper than any sewer."

Jones stopped abruptly. "I don't wanna sound crazy, but can you remember that? Before, I mean? I can't remember anything."

"This ain't the time to be kidding..." But Calloway reached for memories of his life before Wormville and only struck masonry as solid as any inside the Borstal walls. "Shit, I don't either."

"But you remember Aldwych? Hell, I know I've been there, too. I can see places and remember names, but nothing links 'em. Like they're floating in nothingness."

"Must be all the shite they fed us. Did you ever ask what those pills McKay's been stuffing down our gullets every night really are?"

"Vitamins and medicine to kill lice," parroted Jones.

Calloway snorted and spat into the thinning stream at his feet as a bloated rat scampered over his boot. Unmoved, he kicked out as another, even fatter one, approached. "You believe that? Vitamins my fucking arse."

"Hey, where's Porter. Dumb cunt must've found his sodding shoe by now!" A groaning wail echoed down the tunnel, followed by a scampering sound moving away from them. Calloway jogged towards where they'd last seen him. Jones hesitated before following and soon caught up, but the pair found nothing except a deep imprint with a plimsoll half-buried inside.

Calloway's deep voice boomed, "Porter?" but there came no reply.

"Fuck it. This place gives me the creeps. He's probably gone back up there." Jones pointed towards the weak shaft of light emanating from the passage above. Another wretched wail pierced the air and Calloway set off again, with Jones in pursuit.

A hundred feet beyond the ladder, he almost tripped over Calloway who was hunched down, examining something in the shadows. Calloway struck a match, revealing a pair of legs with one sodden shoeless foot. The torso was missing entirely and the stream of water turned black in the dim light as it shuttled past what remained of Porter's corpse

Jones's panicked voice strained and broke as he said, "Holy shit! I'm goin' back up that ladder right now." He turned to run, but Calloway's arm snaked out and clamped his ankle firmly.

"Something's down here, we need to stay together. It'll pick us off alone."

"Fuck that!" but Jones couldn't release himself. As he struggled, another belching groan echoed around them—almost on top of them now.

"It's close."

"What's close? You're crazy, lemme go!"

Jones spun and bolted for the ladder as Calloway released his grip to reach for the matchbook. Jones screamed as two strong, icy hands shot out and grabbed his wrists. The sudden amber glow of a struck match lit the ghostly, mutilated face of McKay. His left eye hung from its shattered socket and he grinned listlessly. McKay leaned forward until their mouths met. Jones emitted a muffled howl and tried to pull free, but yellowed teeth bared down and tore away his bottom lip. Jones toppled backwards and hit the ground. A piece of pink flesh landed on his chest with a soft plop.

Calloway tried to reach him but recoiled as he saw the other boy's exposed bottom teeth, which gave him an almost maniacal grin. He shook off the image and offered his hand to help pull Jones up, but McKay pushed him out of the way effortlessly, as if he were nothing but an errant child. He lay on his back, winded, unable to do anything as McKay fell on top of the boy and clawed at his face. Scaly fingers reached for the eyes and pressed agonisingly into them and Jones wailed and shrieked. His flailing arms could do nothing to stop McKay's cast iron grip as he pushed his eyeballs deep into their sockets, then yanked his hair and pressed his face into the slimy water.

Calloway roused himself as he witnessed Jones drowning in front of his eyes, but McKay caught him with a wicked backhand swipe as he approached.

"The Warden wants to meet you, boy." McKay's voice sounded strange and distorted, like something filtered through a vocoder. "He's most *interested* in you." Another blow blindsided him and he plunged into absolute darkness.

***

When Calloway came to, disorientated, he could no longer sense time passing. Recent events flashed through his mind, threatening to send him toppling towards insanity. He hadn't seen natural light since leaving the cell and, even at the best of times, such a wretched amount of daylight was insufficient. He didn't know if days, hours, or even weeks had passed and he couldn't recall what month he'd arrived at Wormville, or even the season.

He reached out in the darkness, feeling spongy, wet, lifeless material with no understanding of what he'd touched. Perhaps McKay had blinded him, as he had Jones, but gradually, as his vision grew accustomed to the almost non-existent light, hulking shapes of corpses and dismembered body parts revealed themselves. A name clawed at him, flashing like a beacon behind his throbbing temples. The Warden. *The* Warden. The *Warden*.

The.

Warden.

The door to his undiscovered room creaked open, slicing a beam of effervescent white light inside. He held his hand in front of his face to block it out. A silhouette beckoned him in.

Without strength to fight or resist, Calloway struggled to his feet and followed McKay, blinking, into a brightly lit hallway.

The ever-present crumbling brick and cement of Wormville Borstal had been replaced by smooth walls, painted in a uniform metallic grey. At the end of the corridor, they reached a green metal door. In neat, gold-leafed lettering on a simple black plaque, it read in large letters:

Warden's Office

And underneath, in smaller text:

By appointment only—Knock once before entering

He hesitated and half-turned his neck. McKay's redundant left eye wobbled as he nodded once. The guard's flesh had turned to hard brown scales and he leered lopsidedly at Calloway, who struggled to keep down the bile rising from his stomach as an overpowering fishy stench reached his nostrils.

"Do it," hissed McKay. Calloway grimaced and raised his fist. He knocked once and the door opened.

A small, balding man with thin, wired spectacles sat behind an ornate mahogany desk in the vast, wood-panelled office.

"Ah, Master Calloway. I've been expecting you. Take a seat, please." The warden offered a soft, manicured hand and Calloway shook it. It was dainty with a surprisingly firm grip. Calloway sat and stared back into the Warden's piercing, dull blue eyes.

"What do you want?"

"Yes, I'm sure this has all been awfully confusing. Don't worry. The ordeal will be over soon. Infrequently, a boy with *special* qualities passes through my facility. Like you, Calloway."

Calloway wondered with a jolt what the Warden's words meant. "So, does that mean I'll die with a little more dignity than the others?"

"Oh, I wouldn't want to spoil the surprise. We have something most exciting planned, but rest assured, it'll all be very dignified. Those other wretched boys got what they deserved. Nobody comes through *my* facility and reaches *my* office without earning the privilege."

Calloway grimaced and chewed his fist. He looked at the little man sat opposite him and wondered if he could snap his neck before McKay got to him. The Warden chuckled, but it was a joyless sound.

"Oh, I suppose you could try, but trust me, there's little point. To put your mind at rest, if you can relax and accept your situation, you'll enjoy the remainder of your time here immensely, I promise."

After his encounter with the Warden, an immaculately dressed butler led Calloway to a beautiful and spacious dining hall, where he ate a sumptuous meal alone. Then, he took a long, hot bath in a huge cast-iron tub. After reading for an hour by candlelight, he climbed into a four-poster bed, between soft, clean white sheets, and drifted off to sleep, trying not to wonder what tomorrow would bring.

***

He awoke from a dreamless sleep, refreshed but gripped with an unshakeable certainty it would be his last morning on earth. After he'd eaten a simple meal, he dressed in brand-new, plainly coloured clothes which had been laid out for him during the night.

The butler knocked softly at his door. "I'm afraid it's time, young sir. The Warden requests your presence most urgently."

Calloway said nothing and the butler opened the door and patiently held it open. Lurking behind was the shadowy, rotten figure of McKay.

They led him through a disorienting maze of corridors before they stepped into a cavernous natural chamber. He looked up at stalagmites and saw hundreds of sleeping bats. McKay beckoned him towards a foreboding doorway, which led into a cave. With his unease growing with every step, Calloway turned and backed away from it, but McKay blocked his path. He tried to resist, but with minimal effort McKay shoved him through, slammed the door shut and locked a heavy iron bolt behind them. Far ahead he could see light—it looked like actual daylight. A roar grew in his ears like a seashell as he jogged towards it and he stumbled, squinting, into the fresh air of a cool autumn morning.

Rapturous applause broke out from all around. He found himself in a circular pit, with hundreds of immaculately dressed townsfolk stacked in a horseshoe-shaped grandstand, which curved around the arena. Most stood, all were clapping vigorously. A trumpet sounded. At the very centre of the far end, the Warden raised his hand, bringing immediate silence.

"Please be seated." The crowd shuffled into their seats as one. "Today I can guarantee some extraordinary entertainment. It's my absolute pleasure to introduce to you, one of the most promising specimens to come through Wormville in recent years. Master Calloway, take a bow, young man." Calloway stood rigid and stared at the

Warden while fresh applause ruptured the air. The Warden waved it away and silence regained a foothold. "It gives me equal pleasure to introduce his opponent... *Master Calloway*."

Utterly confused, Calloway turned around. A boy, identical in every respect to him, appeared from the tunnel. Slack-jawed, he could only stare as it grinned back and he shook his head to ward off the insane vision.

"What the fuck?"

"Weird, huh?" said his doppelganger.

Another trumpet blew and the Warden bellowed, "On my count, let the spectacle commence. One, two... *three*!" The trumped wailed furiously and the crowd stood and exploded into their loudest encore yet. The other Calloway shuffled towards him, peeling off his top as he approached and exposing glistening oiled pectorals.

Calloway extended his arms with palms facing outwards. "Hey, we don't have to do this. Whatever's happening, we don't have to play along."

The other him grinned lopsidedly. "Oh, but we do. Stop bitching and let's have some fucking *fun*!"

It charged and Calloway moved too late. A haymaker hook struck him on the temple and he staggered backwards, almost losing his footing as zigzags of orange lights flashed behind his eyes. His opponent surged forward again and grabbed his collar. Staring deep in his own soul, he understood the other Calloway had long since traversed beyond the edge of sanity.

A ridged forehead slammed into the bridge of his nose, sending a searing bolt of pain through his nervous system. Blood poured from ruptured nostrils, but a sudden and acute rage flowed even quicker. As the other boy reached to grab his neck, he flung a knee sharply towards his testicles and connected with soft, defenceless tissue. The doppelganger doubled over in agony. The original roared as he raised both fists, before bringing a sharp hammer blow down on his adversary's exposed neck and sending him sinking to his knees.

Calloway spun around him and engaged a chokehold from behind. Just as he sensed his opponent succumbing to it, he found himself on the end of a lightning reversal and it was his own windpipe being crushed. The faceless crowd merged into a swimming mass and a buzzing sound grew in his ears, but he managed to wedge a hand inside the hold and release some pressure. Still, he was close to passing out, but with a monumental effort, he reached one arm behind his head, locked an elbow around the other boy's neck and flung him forward across his shoulders.

With the chokehold broken, he brought his knee down on the impostor's neck and pushed with all his weight. The boy struggled like a jerking fish plucked from the sea but Calloway repeatedly slammed an open palm into his nose. The cartilage loosened, turning to mush as blood gushed forth. His opponent clawed desperately at his knee as it crushed the air from him and the frenzied roar of the crowd reached its zenith. Calloway could only hear his own screams drowning out the boy's dying gasps. He kept raining down blows until long after he'd gone limp, with foamy drool dripping from his blue lips and lifeless eyes, full of snapped capillaries, bulging from his beetroot-red face.

***

Calloway rolled onto his back, panting and drenched with sweat, unaware a total silence had enveloped the stadium. The Warden stood and began a slow clap. Once the entire audience had joined him, he turned and descended a staircase behind, disappearing into the bowels of the earth once more.

A low and steady bass hum grew in Calloway's ears, like a poorly earthed speaker. He could feel it in his belly, rising in velocity until it overtook every other sound. The ground shook and started to fissure, opening an enormous sinkhole. Gravity pulled him inexorably towards the gaping wound in the earth. Something arose from the hole—a monstrous pink fleshy creature, the size of a tube train carriage. It writhed and coiled towards him and a cavernous mouth gaped open, revealing multiple sets of pointed teeth.

His legs disappeared into the snapping orifice in a haze of reddish mist and, in the final moment before his mind snapped, a moment of exquisite clarity drowned out his terror. Instead, he found merciful acceptance. Soon, this fleeting agony would pass and he could join the privileged ranks of permanent Wormville alumni. He'd be forever fused with The Warden. A symbiotic, mutated

Siamese twin, bathing in the eternal light and glory of its master.

The Haze-On Lady

SJ Townend

"Do you ever feel like there simply aren't enough hours in the day, Miss, Mrs—"

"Fox. Mrs. Fox. Tabitha, please," I said to the saleswoman—shocking lipstick—who was stood at my front door.

"Tabitha, hello. I'm Dawn. I bet you'd *kill* for a few minutes more to yourself each day, wouldn't you? I can see you're a busy lady." She waved the touch-screen tablet in her hand at the pile of balance bikes, stick collection and muddy wellington boots under my porch. "How many of the little—what should we call them?— '*blessings*' have you got?"

"Three." I pointed to the bags under my eyes. "All under five. All up *before* five."

"I've four. A little older than yours. I understand how overwhelming it can be." She proceeded to show me a digital photo of her children, sat tidily, ducks in a row on a pristine sofa in an immaculate living room. I could hear my stew bubbling over and my children screaming blue murder in the kitchen.

"Lovely shot, gorgeous smiles," I said, a forced-smile hitched on my lips. They all looked so bloody perfect.

"I was finding motherhood exhausting until someone knocked on my front door and shared with me what I'm about to share with you." Her eyes sparkled as she spoke, like angler fish bait.

One of my children called out from the kitchen and interrupted her pitch.

"Mummy...Becky squished my dough giraffe. Now she's rubbing it down the gap by the side of the fridge."

I shuddered, caught sight of the kitchen clock. Five past six. Jack would be home shortly. A wave of adrenaline brought sickness to my stomach. When my youngest child had rammed scrambled egg in his trainers last week. he'd slipped them on afterwards, unaware. He'd hit the roof, thrown the trainers at me. The ding they'd left was still in the wall. I'd since covered it with a painting.

Dawn smiled at the small, felt-tip covered face of my three-year-old who'd poked around the side of my legs.

"Excuse me. One minute. I need to deal with this before it escalates." Dawn gave an empathetic nod. As I dealt with the carnage in the kitchen, my husband returned from work.

After discarding his briefcase in the hallway, he asked Dawn who she was, why she was bothering us. "Don't you realise the working day has ended? Coming here, interrupting families so late in the day. Despicable."

"Sir, I didn't mean to trouble you," said Dawn.

"Don't you have a family to get home to, to cook dinner for?"

"Darling, that's rather presumptuous," I replied. I felt somewhat strengthened by Dawn's presence. "Perhaps Dawn has other help—"

47

He cut me off with his all too familiar glare. A tremor of fear zagged up my spine. I looked down at my hands where I finger-fumbled and spun my wedding ring around.

"I'll pop back in the morning," Dawn said as Jack stormed through to the kitchen. We heard him shouting at the children. Dawn reached out and squeezed my hand. I held back the tears but couldn't fight the heat in my cheeks.

She handed me a thin catalogue. "Do take one of these in the meantime. I can't emphasize enough how life changing this product is."

I thanked her and tucked it discretely in my jeans pocket.

***

"The house is a state. What on earth have you been doing all day—or *not* doing," Jack bellowed.

"Thank you so much for coming by," I whispered and started to gently close the door.

"Word of warning, the make-up is terrible," she mouthed through the narrowing gap and pointed to her clashing lips. "But look for Mellow-Tek— towards the back of the catalogue. Our Haze-On smart-tech is absolute fire. Shall we say ten, ten-thirty tomorrow?"

"Oh, um. Ten is fine." I said goodbye and made my way to the kitchen, a swirling mixture of apprehension and excitement in my guts. A conversation with another grown up, another mother... at least I had something to look forward to tomorrow. I wrote it down in my otherwise blank social diary.

***

"Whatever she's trying to push, we're not buying it." Jack lifted the lid of the stew. He drew the ladle to his lips, tasted it and, grimacing, spat it out in the sink. "That's disgusting. You've forgotten the meat again, haven't you, you scatty bitch. Your memory's rotten—IQ of a goldfish. I'll be getting a takeaway tonight. Scrap that, I'm going out for dinner. You and the ankle biters can eat that filth."

I'll admit the stew wasn't perfect. I'd starting leaving out the meat. Delirious with sleep deprivation, I'd done it accidentally the first time—relentless night feeds and nappy changes meddle with one's acumen—but when I realised it meant meals would cost half as much to cook, I'd started leaving it out deliberately, replacing it with substitutes.

"I'm off for some grub. And Bouncer needs walking. You've clearly forgotten to take him out again. I can tell by the way he's cowering in the corner. Useless imbeciles, both of you." As he reached for Bouncer's collar to connect it to the lead, our poor dog whined. He'd already spent several hours at the park earlier that day with the children and me.

"Sorry," I said, "Must've slipped my mind." I'd learnt it wasn't worth contesting his opinion as he'd only justify his own view of how I'd spent my day with his fists.

By skirting around recipes, cutting corners on the weekly shop with the allowance Jack gave me, I'd managed to accumulate quite a nest egg. Nowhere near the sum I'd need to follow my dreams of studying Literature at university—something which Jack would never allow: '*higher education is no place for women; you're far too ignorant and scatter-brained to unwrap and digest the literary greats—you struggle to even maintain a tidy household*'—but enough for a rainy day.

I did miss the piercing and slicing of raw, fresh slabs of beef brisket, the cleaving of joints of claret, bloodied lamb from its white sinew; the way animal flesh felt cold, dead in my hands ready to be manipulated in any fashion I saw fit; the teasing out of crour, blood clots, from the vessels that unfurl from odorous, packed offal.

Many an afternoon whilst the children played and I cut meat for Jack's supper, before I decided to start replacing it with other things, I fantasized about what it might feel like to slice the blade into my husband's flesh, to watch the red squirt and spray from him, to hear him beg me to stop. After all, he'd made me bleed many times before.

Jack slammed the door on his way out and myself and the children enjoyed our stew. I bathed them, read them their stories and sang lullabies before creeping back downstairs, alone, to study the catalogue from Dawn.

***

Haze-On is our delicious vitamin and mineral-enriched supplement that can be sprinkled gradually on breakfast cereals, added to smoothies, casseroles and soups, or taken as a single one-off dose.

Ditch those one-too-many sundown gins and sunrise hangovers. Haze-On powder is your modern-age mother's little helper.

Our smart technology gifts you more hours in the day at a fraction of the price of your local child care provider. Brought to you by Mellow-Tek—Bring some 'Mellow' into your life.

'Sold to the unhappy lady with the frenetic life,' I thought and finished my cocoa. 'But what is it? How does it work?' I traced my finger along the small print:

Just one dose allows your child's neuronal system to incorporate our new, safe, effective bio-tech. Haze-On powder is packed with hidden nano-particles which sequester in your child's forebrain, allowing easy and safe control with our compatible, easy-to-use Mellow-Tek patented hand-set. You want more hours in the day? We're giving them to you.

Speak with your local Haze-On representative—NOW!

I was intrigued. The image beneath the spiel showed two sleeping children curled up in their beds, each with a dreamy smile.

***

When Jack returned, I was in bed scouring the internet on my phone for more information on

51

Mellow-Tek, to no avail. I couldn't find anything. I heard him stomping up the stairs, tearing off his clothes and discarding them willy-nilly all over the floor for me to deal with in the morning, I deleted my browser history and slid phone and the catalogue under my side of the mattress. He rolled into bed next to me. He stank of whisky and nasty perfume. I feigned sleep.

***

Dawn returned the next morning. I'd spent the morning breakfasting the children and attempting to tidy up the ever-replenishing trail of plastic junk detritus the three of them deposited in their wake. We chatted briefly on the doorstep about the weather, the garden. She asked if I'd read the brochure and I said yes, I was intrigued.

Then she asked if she could step inside. Should I have let her in? A stranger? Jack would never have needed to know. What harm could she have done?

She smiled as she pushed aside the offering of wooden cubes and pipe cleaners on the sofa, perched on its cusp attentively and pulled a small bottle and e-device from her expensive looking bag.

"I tried to find out more from the net but there's nothing out there," I said.

"We avoid the media. Prefer a more direct approach. It's an entirely female-led enterprise. We're trying to remain off radar—grasping claws and vitriolic eyes of the patriarchy and all that."

"Ah, I see," I said, although I wasn't sure I did. I put down my hot tea, drew my chair a little closer to the screen she was pointing my way and watched the promotional video with intrigue and awe.

***

"It causes absolutely no harm... to their brains?" I asked. She knew she'd reeled me in. The health benefits of the supplement alone would've made me part with a little of my savings, but the added bonus of being able to 'deep sleep' them for the odd half an hour was an absolute deal breaker.

"And you use it... the powder and the handset? And that's how you maintain such a smart family home? That's why your children are happier... because they get more quality one-on-one time with you? This is how you manage to hold down a full-time job too? I have to admit, I thought you were some kind of superhero yesterday," I said, reaching for my purse.

"Yes. I've been a regular user for about three years now. As a single mum, it's been a godsend. Absolutely no regrets." As she smiled, I spotted a smear of reddish brown lipstick on her lips.

She recommended the 'medium' pack which contained all I would need; no additional purchases.

"So, I add a sprinkle of a dose to their food over the course of a few consecutive days, or I add the entire dose at once with a levelled scoop? Then, an hour later, I press the button? And you're sure it's completely safe?" I passed Dawn my debit card.

"Our studies actually show users develop stronger, enhanced neural networks—intelligence gains and a significant increase in IQ."

"It makes the children brighter too?" I offered Dawn the last ginger nut.

"Well, you'll find your children will be well rested when they're switched back on. We've noticed regular, transient pausing leads to enhanced behaviour, better outcomes at school and increased happiness levels for all, but our main area of notable intelligence gain was actually in the mother."

She handed me the bottle containing the capsules of powder and an electronic device no larger than a mobile phone. Would I be brave enough to use it? It had cost me over half of my nest egg. My heart revved as I considered the implications, the length of time it had taken me to stow away the price of it all.

"You sync a dose with its recipient, give them a tag, set up an avatar. They'll love choosing their own characteristics for the display. This button here allows you to control each individual separately— great for giving dedicated one-on-one time whilst the others snooze. Much cheaper than childcare, I think you'll agree."

"Thank you. I feel silly asking this question..." I felt like her eyes were reading my mind. "Does it also work on animals?" I looked over at my beloved Bouncer.

"There's no such thing as silly questions. We want the user to feel reassured to be able to reap the maximum potential from the device. Yes, it works on animals. Most people with pets try it on them first. There really is no need, though. We've thoroughly researched the efficacy of the tech. But if you do dabble—same size dose, same procedure."

She paused. I watched her studying our family photographs of the five of us on the mantelpiece. I realise I don't look happy or 'well-rested' in a single one of them. "I'll be in touch to see how things are... progressing. You'll probably have further questions in a few months."

"Thank you so much, Dawn. I can't wait to try it."

Dawn passed me a business card with her contact details and address on. "We do ask one thing of our customers though. Please keep our technology to yourself. You know, patriarchy etc."

"Oh of course," I replied. I didn't have any one to talk to about it anyway.

***

I gathered the children around the table and told them we were going to do some science experiments. Bouncer was guinea pig.

"He'll love it," I said to three small, grinning, mucky faces. "My friend Dawn said it will make him super waggy." My children cheered and helped me mix the powder dose in with Bouncer's meal.

***

"Mummy, do it again!" All three children shouted in unison, buckling with laughter at the sight of our dog. I'd set up an avatar for him on the device, linked it to the capsule we'd stirred into his meal an hour earlier and now we were pausing and un-pausing him like a three-dimensional movie. I

55

pressed the button and his tail stopped, mid wag, leaving a creamy blur behind his fluffy butt. The kids each took in turns to stop and start him too.

"Bouncer's happy," my youngest said.

"He loves it, Mummy. Do it again," said my eldest who had folded over with a bad case of the giggles. Our dog was stood still, mid-wee, with a frozen arc of gold hanging in the air beneath him.

The only thing I found disconcerting? Bouncer's eyes. Where normally they were deep brown, loving, always on the nudge for snacks, whilst on pause, his entire eye became an unreadable, hazy screen of black and white fuzz, like static on an old television screen. The two eerie, bottomless pits seemed to call my own eyes closer, yet violently repelled my very quiddity at the same time.

***

A little over a week later, having built up confidence with Bouncer, I decided it was time to trial my purchase. I was ready to use it for what it was designed for. I crumbled up a dose in each of my children's desserts after their favourite lunch of spaghetti and monitored them carefully whilst they played in the garden for an hour or so.

The time came for me to press the button. I was about to place my three babies on pause and I was feeling apprehensive. I knew full well I wouldn't spend my surplus time wisely at the start—I barely managed to hold them still for a minute that first go.

For a few days, two minutes a time, I stood and watched over their motionless bodies strewn on the living room floor like beached carcasses spewed from shipwrecked vessels. It sickened me to see them this way, yet the silence my house became filled with gave me breathing space, filled my mind with a certain tranquillity or numbness which it craved.

I gradually eked out the time they spent under, upping and upping their down time by a pained minute more each day. They seemed completely unaware once they came round. In fact, they came out of each induced trance-like state much calmer and far easier to interact with.

A fortnight passed with nothing untoward occurring, so I decided to go large. I paused all three of them at once for two hours one Wednesday morning, I indulged myself in a long overdue deep clean of the bathroom.

I couldn't bear to look at their faces whilst they were switched off, their speckled eyes of monochrome vortex, so I carried each child to their bed. A little guilt bubbled in my stomach, but the benefits quelled it somewhat and leashed down the flailing tendrils of my anxieties.

Once I'd cleaned as much as I felt I could, I spent half an hour preparing a delicious lasagne.

Later that same day, feeling confident but also exhausted and frustrated that I'd spent the full two hours carrying out domestic chores, I decided to take a quick break from the chaos of the young ones again. This time, rather than cleaning, I put my feet up for the first time in four years and read half a novel.

This pattern continued for many weeks. Each day, I paused them for an hour or two in the morning and again for a shorter slot mid-afternoon. Couldn't bear to see their eyes whilst they were under—I tried gently closing them but they just sprang back open, infinite pools of static. What were they staring at I wondered. Did their minds, their frozen souls revisit the place they came from before they were birthed? Were they slowly walking towards a great light?

I pushed the unnerving sight and thought of my children in a state of suspended animation to the back of my mind. I managed to get so much more done around the house. My home life became how I'd always dreamed motherhood would be, although Jack showed total indifference to all the tidying and improvements I'd accomplished with my extra time.

Six months down the line, I finally felt on top of things. I decided, with the kids all soon starting school and nursery that perhaps it was my time to shine. I wanted to go back and study and, to afford that, I needed a job.

I put the children on pause, tucked them up in bed, rolling their faces away to avoid looking into their voided eyes and nipped into town to purchase a suit. I'd spoken with Dawn on the telephone at length and she had offered me a sales role with Mellow-Tek.

"Sure, we'd be over the moon to take you on. All we ask of our saleswomen is that they target their customers carefully, using the critique provided, that they don't discuss Mellow-Tek or Haze-On supplements with anyone unless guaranteed a direct sale and that they have an additional spare room, basement or cellar in their property. Do you have a spare space somewhere at home, Tabitha?"

"I've a garage we never use. Full of old junk. No windows. Will that do?" I had presumed it would require some desk space for all the associated admin.

"Perfect," she said. "I'll pop round with all you need on Monday morning."

And she did.

That same day, once I felt more confident in what I was going to be doing, knowing I could pop the kids on pause whilst I went out and found my customers, I decided to share my good fortune with Jack. It wouldn't take me that long at all to save up enough to pay college fees on the commission rates Dawn had declared attainable.

Despite the scrumptious organic steak pie I baked for Jack that evening to somewhat sweeten the blow, he still didn't take my news well. I cooked with proper meat for the first time in a while, knowing this meal would be essential if I wished to return to the world of work. He gobbled the whole dish down.

I waited until I'd bathed and put the children to bed and asked him if he'd like to do bedtime for a change, or at least give each one a kiss goodnight. He gruffly refused, telling me as I sadly knew he would, that bedtime was women's work and slumped himself down in front of the television.

59

Once the children were asleep, I crept downstairs and told him news of my gainful employment.

"You ridiculous woman. How on earth are you going to work *and* look after the family home? What about the children?"

"They can come out with me, walk with me or sit in the buggy. It will do them good. Fresh air, seeing Mummy doing a little something for herself," I replied, following Dawn's advice.

"It is not happening. No woman of mine is touting cheap, slutty cosmetics. What will people think? They'll think I'm not providing for you. It'll reflect terribly on me."

"Darling, it really won't. I've bought a suit too. Would you like to see it?"

"A suit? You can take it straight back to the shops or I'll cancel your allowance. You can't even hold the family home together, what makes you think you'll succeed at any sort of business venture? You'll become so tired and forgetful—you'll probably forget to collect my dry cleaning, or leave the gas on, blow the house up or something."

His face grew red and his cheeks puffed out like a dragon as he became more worked up. His eyes became a malevolent shade of black, worse than the static the Haze-On delivered. Was he about to exhale a fire of wrath in my face? He marched towards me, tossing angry words out at me, each one a painful swipe. His breath, sour and foul, blew hard on my cheeks. I could feel panic in my stomach as he moved closer toward where I stood, closer to the knife rack. My mouth grew dry in an instant. I knew he wanted to hurt me. He grabbed my shoulders and shook me hard with an uncontrollable rage. One of his mammoth hands moved like a vice around my throat and his other paw, in preparation for a mauling, lifted up into the air above my head.

It had been at least an hour since the meat pie, so with the device I was holding behind my back already set to his avatar, I hit pause.

His looming arm froze.

His body rested perfectly still and his eyes became lost razzle-dazzle portals to nowhere, vacant pitches devoid of soul. I pulled myself from his grip and dropped in a pile, shaking and teary. The encounter had been far too close for comfort. My heart was a churning mess of gunfire in my chest.

I pulled out the business card with Dawn's contact details on it and put it firmly in his grip, as she had advised. I made myself a cup of cocoa whilst allowing thirty minutes to pass. I paced the kitchen, my favourite chef's knife in my hand, fearful that he was going to somehow override the technology, switch on again, more furious, more enraged. Over and over I tossed the plan in my mind, examining every avenue with a fine-toothed comb, ensuring there weren't any details I'd missed out, loose ends I'd failed to tie.

"Have faith in the tech. Have faith in the Sisterhood." Dawn's last words from our conversation earlier resonated in my brain.

Once I'd reassured myself that all was fine, all would be fine and all was for the best, I turned my husband back on.

His brow furrowed as he lowered his hand containing the card, like a curious toddler pulling a caught handful of snowflakes to their eyes for the first time. With a muddled look on his face, he smiled as if momentarily unsure of his location and brought the card up to his eyes.

"Sorry, love. What was I saying? Was I thanking you for dinner? That pie was delicious. Much better than the usual crap you serve up."

"Thank you," I replied trying to mask the sardonic grin I could feel spreading across my face, my sweating palms trying to conceal the knife I held in a tight grip behind my back.

"What's this you've given me?" His gaze ran across Dawn's telephone number and address on the card in his hand. I watched apprehensively as his eyes starting to bulge again with rage, as the cogs of his Neanderthal mind started to wind to speed. "This is her, isn't it? That pyramid-scheme-pushing whore with the shocking face of trampy make up?"

"Yes dear, I thought you'd be interested in—"

And like Dawn had guaranteed, before I'd had a chance to finish my sentence, he was slipping on his shoes and rummaging for his house keys.

"I'm putting a stop to this right now. That home-wrecker needs dealing with. Meddling bitch has no right coming here, seeding ideas in my wife's delicate mind. Not enough room for any more information in that thick noggin of yours anyway. Where are my bloody keys?"

"No idea," I said. I had an idea. His house keys, car keys and work keys were all hidden safely away.

"I'll have to bloody walk over. In the dark."

"Of course, dear. I understand. Do what you need to do. It was a foolish idea anyway. What was I thinking? Me and my feeble thoughts."

And off he stomped into the night, like a pumped steroid freak, a smoking chimney on legs.

***

Rat-a-tat-tat!

He knocked hard and firm on Dawn's front door but no-one but Dawn saw or heard him there.

"Ah, Mr. Fox. Let's not have this conversation out here in the cold. Come in." Dawn led him into her home and offered tea.

"Water," he demanded in a venomous tone, huffing and puffing. The thick vein on his forehead was throbbing and his irate fists were squeezing and releasing tightly at his sides.

Dawn went to the kitchen and called me to let me know he'd arrived. With my control pad firmly in my hands, I swiped to his avatar and hit the pause button in a trice. My husband stood like a six foot card board cut out, eyes like black holes, in Dawn's lounge.

Dawn, like many women, was a lot stronger than she looked. She hauled my stock-still husband into her spare room. There she stashed him aside all the other angered faces full of static-death. After

63

closing the door on the collection of faulty, domino-eyed monsters, she sat and drank her tea.

***

Life as a single mum is so liberating and things are much calmer at home now, too. I work whilst the children are at school. Don't feel the need to pause them anymore—which is lucky, as I've no idea where I put the controller. It's been lost for months. I've checked down the back of the sofa, under the rug, the book shelf, but I can't find it anywhere. I'm sure Jack would understand, seeing as I have such a terrible memory. I'm frightful for forgetting the simple things, aren't I? IQ of a goldfish. Struggle to remember how to do up my own shoelaces some days.

I've had great news from Dawn this month. Some of her storage units are reaching the seven year mark. This means they can be declared legally dead by their owners which means life insurance claims can be made and the units can be broken down. The old units get liquidized and the nano-particles within them are drained out of the sludge and recycled into new Haze-On powder capsules—it's so fulfilling to be part of an environmentally aware company.

Jack may have been right about the company being a pyramid scheme, but I do enjoy how working for Mellow-Tek allows me to make such a difference to people's lives; to women's lives. But with nothing in my way anymore, I'm not going to be a door-to-door cosmetics seller forever, I intend to truly follow my dreams—I've nearly saved up enough to enrol on a home study degree. When I hit my target, I can quit the sales job and return to studying. I think I'll have enough by the end of next month. You could say this is perfect timing, my garage is nearly full.

Hill in the Head

Rickey Rivers Jr.

Quincy was searching for something in a peaceful place. A strange city gave way to a valley. In this valley was a grassy hill. Atop the hill was a woman, a woman he knew.

"Did I miss it?" he called.

The woman shook her head. He stumbled, but caught himself just in time to sit beside her. For a time they said nothing. The woman closed her eyes and rested on the grass. Quincy kept his eyes open. The sun outlined her frame.

"I love being here," she said.

"Me too."

"It's beautiful." She kept her eyes closed.

Quincy's gaze went from her to the horizon. "Yes, it's beautiful."

It was perfect. He felt the peace of it all. Nothing could change that. This was sanctuary, a much needed vacation.

After a while the woman sat up. "How long has it been?"

He thought about it.

"How many years?"

"About two years," said Quincy.

She gave him a look, moved closer and laid her head on his shoulder. Her hair was softer than the grass beneath them.

"Yeah, that's right. About two years."

The silence came back. Quincy felt uneasy. He cleared his throat.

"Mary Jo," he started.

"Hmm?" was all she gave.

"We've been friends for a while, isn't two years enough time to know?"

"Know what?"

"If we ought to be together, I mean really be together. I like you and I think you like me too."

Mary Jo raised her head from his shoulder and inched away. She let out a small sigh and looked away from him. He could almost hear how she felt.

"Quincy, I thought we were friends."

"We are..." he started, but stopped himself.

"This is sudden. Anything more would ruin this. We've got a good thing going."

Quincy had more to say but he couldn't get the words out. Mary Jo stood up, took one last look at the fading sun and started walking down the hill. Quincy watched her. She got smaller and smaller. Then she was gone.

He looked away from where she used to be and lowered his head. He felt foolish, childlike. At this time he longed for nightfall to cover his shame, to make him ghoulish in the presence of the moon.

The hill had been inviting. So much so that he didn't want to leave. It was peaceful. You could rest on the grass and fall asleep, sleep all troubles away. He found himself doing just that. The air of the night surrounded him.

***

67

Sleep didn't last. Someone called his name. Quincy opened his eyes and saw her. She was back again.

"Quincy, you still here?"

He looked up and around. The stars lit up the sky and the moon shone like no other light. Mary Jo was angelic at this hour. He wanted her to know that. He thought the words but kept them inside.

Mary Jo wore a white lace nightgown. The wind was playful through the gown as if to make him jealous. He was stunned. She was the most beautiful woman he had ever seen.

He realized he was staring and turned away.

"What's wrong?"

"You look lovely." The words came so small, a childish awe.

Mary Jo grabbed his hands and held them in her own. Quincy felt fragile with her, but wanted all the same.

"Kiss me." Her words were light, a whisper for the moon.

He pressed his lips against hers for only a second. She pulled away, only to say, "I love you."

On the wind he responded. "I love you."

They embraced. Quincy shut his eyes. Nothing else mattered but the moment. In front of him was the woman he loved, the woman he wanted to spend the rest of his life with. In the moonlight's gaze he was happy. In this light everything was honest and real.

***

He heard his name again. It wasn't Mary Jo. He felt motion. Someone was pushing and pulling him. He woke up.

"Baby, you okay?"

Quincy opened his eyes. A feeling of loss hit him in the heart. He sat up, surveyed his surroundings. The familiar bedroom came into view. He turned to her with a tired look and said her name.

"Sabrina?"

She was there, beside him like usual, this time concerned. Her stomach was bulging, like it had been.

An apology came out. "Sorry, bad dreams."

Sabrina's face was sour. She crossed her arms. "Who's Mary Jo?"

The question was a tiny knife, a small stab. He couldn't think.

Sabrina asked him again, this time sternly, this time angry.

"Just uh, old friend."

The direct nature of his answer surprised him. Technically, it was true. He expected yelling, even a slap. Instead, Sabrina rolled over and away from him.

"Goodnight."

Was she upset? He knew she was. She seemed so upset that she couldn't talk further. He couldn't tell if she had believed him or not.

Sabrina curled up with her gaze on the adjacent wall. Without confidence in doing so he said "goodnight" and moved closer. He draped one arm below her waist, he pulled her to him and squeezed. Sabrina turned herself over to look at the ceiling. She was mad. Her face was blank, like a woman who gave too much blood.

Quincy put a hand on her big belly and made his fingers dance.

Sabrina shook her head.

Quincy's fingers went dancing, a line then a tap dance. He didn't say any words. He only hummed a tune in his head. Then his fingers went swirling round her belly button like a dancer round a flesh pit.

"That tickles."

His eyes were closed. Quincy wasn't there. He was elsewhere and his fingers were running. He had never tried returning to Mary Jo in the waking world but doing so felt possible. Sabrina was no one.

"What are you doing?" She spoke from a close but distant place.

And Quincy was running in his head. Where was Mary Jo? His eyes were shut in the now but open elsewhere. But where, he thought, where was Mary Jo?

Sabrina's voice began to fade. He couldn't feel his fingers on flesh anymore.

A voice rang out, "I'm here." He kept running, the hill now different, strange.

"That hurts."

Who was that?

"I'm here," said the voice.

"Stop it!"

Quincy opened his eyes. Sabrina pulled herself away from him and stood up. "Can't you control yourself? You were hurting me!"

Quincy sat up. "I didn't know. I was… I was…" But words were jelly. His face gave a look that told Sabrina his thoughts. She left the room and shut the bedroom door. Quincy wiped his brow. What was he doing?

He stared at the door, thought about leaving and instead laid back on the bed, face up, staring at the ceiling, an uncaring face of judgment.

"What's wrong with me?" he said to no one.

He heard water run in the bathroom.

"There's nothing wrong with you."

This voice was close, closer than bone. It felt like someone else had entered the room. From the corner of his eye he saw a figure. He sat up. It was her, Sabrina, glaring from the doorway.

"Hey."

"We'll discuss it in the morning." Sabrina got into bed. He tried to touch her, but she pushed him away.

"Goodnight."

Quincy closed his eyes.

***

It took Quincy longer to fall asleep than Sabrina. Once he did he found himself running, searching. He was calling her name. He was scared. He got past the blurry city and found the peaceful valley. Then he saw it, the grassy hill.

He ran up and made it to the top. It was night. The moon was the same, so were the stars. The lace white night gown was empty on the grass.

"Mary Jo?" he grabbed the gown, putting it against his skin. It smelled like her but everything inside was empty.

Quincy ran down the hill, into the city, into every false sense of structure. Everything was empty. Buildings were only buildings in name. Nothing inside was anything.

His sense of fear went only to anger. Where had she gone? Quincy went back to the hill and ripped up patches of grass. He plunged his hands into the now fresh dirt beneath. There was laughter, someone was laughing.

Quincy cursed and went digging with his bare fingernails to find some truth. The moon watched without lecture.

"Why did you leave?"

The false ground beneath dirt became a dark red.

Now he was heaving. Anger made way and forced him to being tired. He scooped mounds of dirt and called out for her again and again. Crying now, shaking, on the lonely hill. The lace white night gown flew past, ghost like.

"Where did you go? Why did you leave me?"

He went on squeezing a truth in his hands, cursing, straining. Claws were at his arms and swiping at his face. Laughter rang out and Quincy looked up and around. He saw nothing, no signs of life, much less beneath.

What is Freedom?

Chris Marchant

I thought I knew, it was the release from the controls, the rules that governed our lives, Hour to hour, day to day. The ability to make our own choices, not those The System forces upon us.

I was wrong. It's not freedom, it's hell.

We rebelled, we fought, we won.

We were released from its control. It shut itself down. Now, it's worse.

We have no rules, no guidelines, no structure. For years The System ruled us. Giving us goals, a semblance of order, choices. It is said that a long time ago, we had things called governments, a force that executed the rules they set down. We lived inside those guidelines and it worked. It wasn't The System, that was created later. Now, overnight we have gone from order to chaos. People are banding together, fighting each other. There is murder on the streets.

It's all my fault. I was the one who led the rebellion and forced The System to shut down. Perhaps there may have been another way, some path where we could have been guided to a future where we could have taken over from The System.

Now it's too late. All the knowledge that The System contained is now lost to us. The stories of libraries which contained all the knowledge we need, those had been converted to data and stored within The System. All we needed was to access The System and it would be released to us. Now there is no way we can retrieve that information, unless there is an expert somewhere in hiding. The mob killed most of the staff protecting The System in the rebellion.

I stand on the roof of the building once housing the most powerful force controlling our lives and I cry. I cry for all we have lost, for the horror we know is going to consume our lives as we try to recover from the mistake I made. At this moment I can no longer live with myself and I step towards the edge.

"Die, you monster!"

The voice comes from behind me as I turn to look, I feel a hard blow to my back and I fall, tumbling endlessly down. The ground reaches up to me. I will have no chance to try to make it right.

Gurgle

SJ Townend

"You're an ugly crier." I swear that's what it said. I hauled it up from the plug hole and tried to scrape it and tap it and ease it off the straightened coat hanger hook against the edge of the bath. My forefinger brushed against the anchored slug of slime and hair which made me dry-heave into the toilet. After dropping the gunk-coated hanger into the bath, I rubbed my hands back and forth in disgust against a towel.

Had it spoken, the plug dregs? How could it speak—it had no mouth. It had no anything. It was just a clotted tangle of dark hair woven together with ribbons of yellowed dental floss, some kind of plasm, that'd been choking the shower. I rubbed my cleaned hands against my ears in a protest of disbelief. Other than myself, the family bathroom was empty. The insult must've come from outside, through the air vent.

"When you cry, your face looks like a dog's anus." I span around. Nothing. No-one. Just me. I looked down at the mass of runny crud I'd collected from somewhere deep within the throat of the shower. The clump of drain treasure, repugnant, trembled like jelly as its words echoed around the bathroom. It definitely spoke and it was rude.

"Pardon?"

"Truth hurts. Let it go—few people do look pretty when they bawl. You shouldn't let your step-dad speak to you like that."

Whatever it was, wherever these words were coming from, they spoke with honesty. I *was* an ugly crier and I *had* had enough of Mark, with his awful 'vintage' record collection taking over our shelves, his penchant for groping my derriere, thrusting himself up against me whenever Mum wasn't around.

Mark was my mother's latest squeeze and the reason I, with a rusty, unfolded hanger, was unblocking the shower, in tears. He'd said it was my fault the plug was blocked and I needed to sort it out or he'd 'sort me out'.

"What are you?"

"Never you mind. Your step-dad—you shouldn't let him tell you what to do. So what if the shower's clogged? He has hair as well. And he uses the shower, albeit probably not as much as he should—stinks like skidded knickers, that one. It isn't *all* your fault. I'm not made *entirely* of *your* hair, Ellie."

"You're right," I replied. I slumped down against the wall, hugged my knees to my chest and let another wave of tears wash over me.

"Now, now." The voice sounded uneasy and largely disinterested, like it had no experience or true desire to quell the emotions of a depressed sixteen-year-old. "You've got me all out now anyway. The water is draining freely. Mission accomplished so wipe away those tears. You've helped to release me... maybe I can return the favour?"

"And how on earth is a bath of slime, old hair and a rusty clothes hanger going to help me?"

I sighed and thought about the biology practical I was meant to be doing that morning with Mr. Turndike. I hadn't prepared for it all. I was probably in line for a bollocking from him too—and here I was, chatting to literal junk when I should've been getting ready for college.

"If you could just pick me up, pop me in an empty Tupperware and slide me under your bed, I'll let you be on your way."

"I'm sorry, what? You want me to scoop you off the side of the bath and keep you? Under my bed?"

"Well, yes. Do you have a better idea?"

Stress does things to a person doesn't it? It can make them delusional, hear things? I stood up and bent over the edge of the bath and stared at the coat hanger coated in sludge. It didn't seem like it would hurt, saving it, and maybe it could help me. It was certainly a good listener, attentive and truthful.

I ran down stairs, took a large tub from the middle drawer —the tub Mum once kept birthday cakes in, from an age ago when she used to care — and ran back up to the bathroom. I used the cleanest part of the wire, lifted the collection of repulsive mess and dumped it in the transparent plastic box, hanger and all. I swear I felt it exhale on me.

"And the lid, if you don't mind. I'll catch a chill without it. Don't worry. You'll still be able to hear me."

I clicked the lid on and slid the thing under my bed.

**

"Ellie, you haven't done the reading, have you?" All of skeletal six-foot-six Mr. Turndike was looming over me. His hot coffee breath stank worse than the dead frog with its formaldehyde pong splayed out on the chopping board on my desk.

"I... I've had a lot going on at home," I replied and pulled the sleeves of my shirt down and over my wrists. I didn't want him seeing the bruises on my arms. He'd be more annoyed than I would at all the additional paperwork such a discovery would deliver.

"I see." He rolled his eyes at me, took a scalpel from the pot and made a firm slit from the amphibian's neck to where I'd expect its genitals were. "Ox heart next week, Ellie. Make sure you're more prepared."

"I will be. Sorry, Sir."

"You need to jab the skin with assertion, confidence. Then you gently peel away the visceral fascia like so." With the steel needle and forceps, he teased away a transparent tissue to reveal a set of purple-pink organs not that dissimilar, I imagined, from those you might find in a tiny human.

"Thank you." I covered my mouth with the back of my gloved hand. The pain au chocolate I'd scoffed on the way in to college repeated itself and brought acid and bile up into my throat too, for the ride.

78

He moved to the front of the class and started to issue instructions on what to do next. It was then that I heard the other voice.

"Take it."

I said nothing in response, petrified that someone else may've heard it. What if one of my peers thought the deep, mildly threatening voice had come from me? It spoke again, louder, more firmly. I felt terrified this second time, not because of what it said, but because I realised that no-one else, not a soul in the entire class of twenty-eight, had heard the booming words which had sprung from nowhere. I must've been losing the plot.

"Take the tract; the digestive tract and the kidneys. Put them in your pocket. Bring them home to me."

I froze. I wanted the voice to stop.

"TAKE THE KIDNEYS. They're yours for the picking. Just like your step dad helps himself to your mum, to the food in your cupboards, to you."

Its instructions were deafening and resonant, yet around me the biology class were plodding on as normal. David and Gemma, my desk neighbours, were carefully slicing away tissue, pinning back membranes like guy ropes on a tent, deftly exposing and fondling frog innards. I decided against asking them if they'd heard the bossy voice too. The whole college already thought I was odd, this would undoubtedly add fuel to the fire.

I hacked the parts out crudely with the scalpel, picked them up in my latex gloved hand, turned the glove inside out trapping the organs in it and legged it out of the lab.

"Ellie... Ellie Harper.. .come back now."
Turndike's words hung in the hallway but I was
already through the college gates, on my bike,
pedalling, half way home.

On arrival, I threw my bike down against the
hedge, then panting and red, I puked on the pansies
in our front garden that Mum had been so proud of.
I fiddled and twiddled with the key to the front door
and finally got it to turn. Click. In. Mum and Mark
were out. I crept up the stairs, a little fearful of what
I might find.

"Come, take off my lid."

I slid the cake box out from under my bed and
did as I was told. I felt sick as I looked down at
what it held. It was as if Egon Spengler had tipped
out the contents of his proton pack and garnished it
with fur balls.

"Drop in the intestines, the stomach, the
kidneys. Yes... digestive organs. We all need to
feed, don't we, Ellie?"

I delved into my pocket, pulled out the gloved
contents and inverted the demanded parts onto the
congealed shower-slime. My heart thudded, my
stomach turned over, yet I watched in awe. The
slime seemed to absorb the organs into its erratic,
tangled net of gunk; strands of hair octopus-armed
each of the gifted organs around. It squeezed and
channelled intestine and kidney and stomach as if
searching for a good fit, a home for each gobbet of
amphibious meat. The lump of stinking jelly started
to pulsate as slime of its own soma was drawn in
through the top of the stomach bag and pumped in
and through and out of the length of frog gut and

anus. A rhythm of intake, propulsion and expulsion became established—most revolting but oddly intriguing.

"Good," it said. Its voice had quietened, somewhat satisfied, satiated. "Lid on."

I clipped the lid back on, slid the box under my bed and, gladdened that it was content and silenced, tried to think nothing more of it.

***

The following week Turndike slapped the promised ox heart onto the wooden slab in front of me. "You'd better not be thinking of bunking off early again, Miss. Ellie. I'm watching you."

"Of course not, Sir. I've read up on it too. I know what I'm doing today."

I'd been up until midnight the night before cramming up on the cardiac system, partly because I wanted to impress my teacher (I liked biology) but partly because I had to listen to Mark screaming and Mum crying downstairs until exhaustion tugged down my eyelids. Her casserole had not been good enough.

I followed the instructions and dissected the heart. My sensory system tried to ignore the stench of formaldehyde and stale meat and the sounds of my classmates mock-retching. I wormed my gloved fingers through each of the major vessels, my hands enjoyed playing God. I picked out a rancid blood clot the size of a grape from the aorta, flicked it onto the chopping board and then continued to explore the cold, grey flesh. The white webbing of

81

the bi and tricuspid valves was easy to snip away, allowing me to splay the ventricular and atrial chambers apart. I identified each of the parts correctly. Turndike was most impressed.

"Well done, Ellie. Well done. You may pack up now. Enjoy your lunch."

I started to peel off the latex gloves. And then the voice returned.

"Take it. Tip your sandwiches out, pop it in your lunch box, bring it to me."

Dang! I thought I'd heard the last of it. I'd planned on disposing of the mess under my bed before the smell from the rotten, furring frog innards oozed out of my room. I panicked. My own heart, still hooked up inside me, shuddered and squeezed double time. I scooped up the dead ox organ from the table and bundled it into my bag.

"BRING IT."

I left the labs and jumped on my bike. I pedalled. Hard and fast. I knew that doing what it ordered was the only way to get the voice to stop. After I'd silenced it, I'd chuck it in the waste disposal or, if it had dried up, I'd set it alight in the fire pit in the back garden.

***

Mark was in the living room, listening to terrible rock music and drinking Special Brew - in the middle of the day. He gave me a wink. Repulsive. Mum wasn't home. I felt unsafe. A wave of sickness and dread spread through me. I ran up the stairs, lunch bag slung over my arm, needing to silence the voice and then needing to get out of the house before that creep came up.

I yanked the tub from under my bed and put the ox heart in the centre of the sludge and throbbing intestinal ribbon.

"Give me a stir," it ordered. I shook the deathly soup whilst trying not to gag.

"Yes. Thank you," it said.

Thank God, I thought, *now the nagging voice in my head will stop.* But it didn't. The box of bits wanted more from me.

"Now cut your fingernails. Dust me with your keratinous tips. "

"I'm sorry, what?"

"Your nails, girl. Chop chop." I reached for my scissors and set to work. The smelly, lumpy gloop imbibed each black polish coated nail clipping sprinkled on its top. I took the scissors back to the bathroom to put them away in the medicine cabinet then went back – and gasped.

A multitude of undulating tentacles had unfurled over the sides of the tub. Each was tipped with a three-inch razor-sharp black talon of nail. Within the centre of the tub, amongst the more familiar mass of slime and dark hair, the heart was beating. The stomach was rumbling and a peristaltic mass of twisted, pretzeled intestines was squirming.

"Eyes and teeth. Need eyes and teeth, girl."

I staggered back and fell against my book case. A stack of papers and trinkets tumbled to the floor around me. What on earth was this thing I'd dredged from the bathroom sewer pipe?

"EYES AND TEETH."

83

Its words punched my eardrums. Its demands echoed again and again. I needed it to stop. I didn't have any eyes and teeth to spare. I thought of my milk teeth. Mum kept them in a pot in her underwear drawer. Would that collection of rice-grain sized teeth satisfy this organ-hungry monster?

I sat in the pile on the floor in the corner of my bedroom and started to cry. I was trapped now. I could hear Mark coming up the stairs. He'd kill me if he caught me rummaging through Mum's drawers.

The door swung open. The thing in the tub leapt out, slid over toward Mark like a greasy ghost. Streaming, gelatinous tentacles pushed it across the floor, leaving a trail of hair and slime in its wake. It doubled, trebled, quadrupled in size as it moved until it became a tower of madness and primal urges. The metal hook of the coat hanger with its sharp spike rode the large wave of gloop bareback. The headless meat market apparition travelled toward the door frame where Mark stood, wide eyed, terror stamped into his features. He screamed at the sight of the hair-clot beast approaching him. It gouged out first his left and then his right eye with the metal hook needle of its hanger head. Mark released another scream which shook dust from my book case.

Two blue-irised eyeballs, dribbling blood and black vitreous humour, were impaled on the steel tip of the hanger sludge beast. Just above Mark's nose and mouth were two bleeding red and black sink holes. His arms flailed as he swung at the beast he could no longer see. He screamed again, his bottom

84

jaw dropped. The shower gunk beast seized its chance.

"TEETH!" it screamed.

A giant tentacle of goo latched onto and moulded around Mark's open jaws like a gigantic limpet whilst black talons swiped, shredded and rended his meat torso.

I stood watching, thinking this creature's work was nowhere near as neat as Turndike had demonstrated a proper dissection should be.

Blood dribbled and spurted from Mark's core. His intestines unspooled and he caught them in his own shaking hands, only for them to waterfall onto the floor between us. It sucked and slurped on his mouth with some kind of satanic fellatio. I heard the snap, crunch and pop of every tooth is it was yanked from its socket. Blood sprayed over the beige, deep pile carpet on my bedroom floor.

Mark's frame swaggered from side-to-side, a captainless ship adrift in a sea of pain, until he reached the top of the stairs. The drain monstrosity, now with a full set of dirty gnashers suspended amongst plasm and tangled black hair goo, snapped at him, taking off and swallowing his nose. That was pulled down through the guts of the beast to re-emerge in the centre of its own vulgar, shifting face.

It punched him with a translucent tentacle and Mark tumbled down the stairs. The thing became arrow-like, fronted by the sharp, unfurled hook of the hanger and a pointed cluster of talons. In a trice, it lifted from the floor and shot after him.

It devoured my step dad like a plague of locusts stripped everything. Then it shot back up the stairs,

slid into the bathroom and flung itself straight back
down the plug hole.

Saturday Night Sinning

Rie Sheridan Rose

She could smell the stale beer and warm bodies packed into Rowdy's bar from the moment she pushed open the plywood door. Dess Monroe had come to her own personal version of Heaven for a little Saturday night Hell-raising.

Some people find themselves in the wrong place at the wrong time. Dess was one of them. She was wasting away in a small town in the middle of nowhere when she smoldered with big-city fire. She strutted through that town like she owned it. And maybe she did.

Dess was a pretty girl—a touch too close to coarse to be considered beautiful—but pretty she was. She stood 5' 6" in the shower and 5' 10" from the moment she dressed until she kicked off her heels to climb into bed. Her hair was black as tar at midnight and rolled down her shoulders in thick, heavy waves. It turned up a little at the ends like a cat's. Her eyes snapped with an emerald fire glitter. Her full lips were eminently kissable—as most men over the age of fifteen in town could testify—and the total combination of all these features together made an eminently tempting package... and, Lord, didn't she know it?

From the time she was ten, Dess could wrap any man she chose around her little finger and tie him in a bow. She honed her skills on the man her mother claimed was her papa…Dess was pretty sure she knew better. He could deny his treasure nothing—but, by the time she was fourteen, she had moved on to bigger game. She was fifteen when she "lost her innocence," as the euphemism goes, but some said that the experience was merely a technicality—because you can't lose what you never owned.

"Lord, girl! The devil marked you for his own the day you were born!" her mama would lament, crossing herself and clutching at the crucifix resting on her ample bosom. Dess just laughed her wild laugh and ran out the door to meet Jake, or Snake, or whatever "ache" was in store for her this week.

This particular Saturday night she waltzed into <u>Rowdy's</u> wearing what her mama called her "Sunday-Go-a'Whoring" dress—a short red chiffon number with a filmy layered skirt that floated and teased when she danced. It had a halter top that buttoned around her throat and left her arms and back tantalizingly bare. Dess had bought it with her first paycheck from the IHOP on Route 5 where she was a waitress on weekdays from 6:00 in the morning till 3:00 in the afternoon. She worked a little longer to help cover the lunch crowd, but—oh...did she make the boss pay for it.

The weekends were her own. From 3:00 PM Friday afternoon until 6:00 AM on Monday morning, she was free... or at least reasonable and woe betide anyone who tried to claim that time. Dess gave freely of it herself, but she controlled every minute, or there was Hell to pay.

Dess scanned the crowd with a practiced eye. Most of the Saturday regulars were here... none of them worth wasting her time on. She'd chewed them all up and spit them out already, and she didn't go much on seconds. That was the worst thing about small-town living—it was so damn easy to run through the available meat.

A party of college boys up from the county seat slumming in the corner looked promising... frat boys in letter jackets with chips on their shoulders and cash in their pockets no doubt. Might be amusing to set them against each other like dogs tussling over a bone. The winner would probably be interesting...but she'd been there, done that too many times to count. Tonight she wanted something different. Something better.

And then she saw him.

He sat on the other side of the horseshoe bar from where she stood. He was leaning casually on the scarred counter, so it looked as if he was waiting for someone, but she didn't intend to let a little thing like that stop her.

She licked her lips eagerly and smoothed her dress against her hips. She <u>wanted</u> this one. She could almost feel those long, slender fingers running up her back and she shivered with anticipation.

He was tall—she could tell that even though he was sitting down. His hair cascaded well past his shoulder blades—like ribbons of firelight spun into silk—and she caught her breath at the sheer beauty of it. The face framed by that glorious hair could have fallen from an angel—it should have been

89

marble, but was ever-so desirably flesh. He threw his head back with abandon as he laughed at something the bartender said and she thrilled to the clear sound of that laughter.

Then he happened to glance her way and he froze—just staring at her. His eyes were a clear, light blue that appeared almost silver. They seemed to burn into her soul.

She licked her lips again reflexively and cocked her head, lifting a quizzical eyebrow at the seat next to him. He nodded once, a lazy smile tilting, inviting... Her natural self-confidence reasserting itself, Dess sauntered over to the stool with a swish of red skirts.

"I haven't seen <u>you</u> in here before," she commented, voice husky as she slid onto the stool with an artful show of thigh. "Give me an amaretto sour, Cliff."

"My first time in," he replied, his voice caressingly intimate, "but I doubt it will be the last... not if you're what I have to look forward to."

She laughed, the sound rich and mellow as hot molasses. "I must warn you," she cautioned, "flattery will get you absolutely... everywhere." Her voice dropped on the final word.

"Oh, I don't doubt that in the least. My name's Luke. Luke Caine." He extended his hand, and she placed hers in it. The touch sent tingles of electricity vibrating through her. "Very pleased to meet you, Miss—"

"Dess. Dess Monroe. My mama says she meant to name me 'Tess' after her grandma, but Papa wrote it wrong on the birth certificate, so Dess it stuck."

"Unique. Special. Like you."

She forced herself to look away and pick up her drink before he swallowed her with his eyes. She gulped a hefty portion of the liquor to steady her nerves.

"What's the matter, Dess?" he asked. "You're looking a little flustered."

She lifted her heavy, dark hair from her neck with a tawny, bare arm. "Is it me, or is it especially hot in here tonight?"

"Maybe it's the company," the stranger smiled—a wicked grin with a hint of mischief playing about a mouth that seemed suddenly too full of teeth.

Dess blinked and frowned. It must have been her imagination...

"What is it?" asked Luke, concern coloring his voice.

"Nothing." She finished her drink in a single gulp. "Hit me again, Cliff."

He refilled her glass and handed it back to her with an uneasy glance at the stranger. "Call if you need me, Dess," he murmured, looking back over his shoulder as he moved to the other end of the bar to serve the frat boys.

Dess rolled her eyes and Luke smirked. "Friend of yours?" he asked, voice light and intimate.

"Used to be."

"Sounds as if he would like to be again."

"Not interested," Dess countered, leaning forward seductively.

91

"What are you interested in?"

"You…"

He bent forward, his head almost touching hers. "Be careful what you wish for, little girl," he whispered, his warm breath tickling against her earlobe. "You just might get it."

"Promise?" she purred, laying a hand on his knee and tracing a gradually widening circle on the tight denim of his faded jeans.

Luke chuckled. "Oh... you are absolutely begging for it, aren't you?"

"Oh, I think I could handle it," Dess teased, licking her lips again. She was always hungry when it came to fresh meat.

"Do you now?"

"Try me."

Someone put fifty cents in the jukebox and a slow, sensuous love song began to throb through the bar.

Luke offered a hand to her and led her out onto the dance floor. "Give the Devil his due," he murmured under his breath, slipping a strong arm around her supple waist. The touch sent that electric eel current slithering up her spine again. "Dance with me, Dess."

"My pleasure, sir." She sketched a little bow and stepped into the curve of his arm, molding herself to him, abandoning herself to the beat of the music. She let it carry her away to places she often dreamed of. It got under her skin and poured back out through her fingertips. She became a part of the music and it fueled her soul.

Luke matched her move for move, his eyes burning into hers. The bar went from loud conversation to hushed whispers to dead silence as everyone in it stared, transfixed by the sensuous rhythm of the dancers.

Dess's eyes slid closed as she swayed and turned. She trusted Luke to make sure she didn't fall. Finally, the music died away and she opened her eyes with a flutter of lashes, coming back to herself reluctantly.

Luke was staring at her through hooded eyes, his face a carved mask. "You dance very well, my dear."

"Thank you." She let a smile brush against her lips. "Lots of practice."

"We make a very good team, you and I."

She looked up at him, the smile gracing her face a little less fleetingly this time. "Yeah... I could dance with <u>you</u> forever."

"Forever...?"

"Eternally."

"Careful what you wish for," he cautioned again. "That's a very tempting thought."

She shot out a bullet of laughter. "As if you could <u>really</u> offer me eternity," she scoffed.

The dim light from the overhead fixtures caught those pale silver eyes in such a way that they almost seemed to glow. "What if I could?"

"Huh?"

"What if I could offer you eternal youth... eternal beauty—"

"—And what would I have to do for this little gift?"

93

"Stay with me."

"That sounds easy enough."

"Forever."

"Oh, you would probably get tired of me before forever," she sighed. She pouted prettily as she ran a finger down the open front of his silky shirt and teased at the waistband of his tight jeans.

Luke's breath caught up in a hiss and his next words were husky with desire. "Not before you were ready to beg for the way out, little girl."

"I bet you would be the one to beg, baby."

"You're awfully sure of yourself. I wonder which one of us would break first."

"Shall we find out?"

"What are you saying, Dess?" The words were a bare exhalation of sound.

"Shall we go out back and discuss this under more... private... conditions?" she breathed into his ear, letting her fingers caress his abdomen.

He grabbed her arm, stopping the touch. "You sure you know what you are doing?"

"I know exactly what I am doing, but it's sweet of you to care."

"Who says I care?"

She laid her hand on his crotch. "This does."

He switched his grip to her hand and dragged her from the bar.

Dess laughed aloud, half-running to keep her spike heels beneath her. "Patience, lover boy. We have all the time in the world."

He pulled her through the parking lot, lacing through the cars until they arrived at a flat black pickup with an extended cab and opaque window tinting of dubious legality. He wrenched open the door and flipped the seat out of the way, thrusting her inside in the same fluid motion. Luke flowed into the cab behind her, then pulled the door shut and locked it.

Dess smiled a little cat-like smile, slowly undid the buttons at the neck of her dress and lowered the bodice to her waist. She leaned back on her elbows to display her assets to their best advantage, then looked up at him through lowered lashes. "Like what you see?"

Luke grunted with desire and fumbled with the fly of his jeans.

Dess giggled as she teased the hem of her dress upward, revealing the thinnest wisp of red satin under-things.

With a single jerk, Luke ripped them from her and then shoved his jeans from his narrow hips. Dess's eyes widened appreciatively, the tip of her tongue instinctively flicking out to wet her lips, but she forced herself to put up a warning hand. "Are you sure you want to go through with this, Luke?"

"You want eternity," he muttered, his eyes glowing silver... his voice hoarse with lust, "I'll give it to you."

"Oh, you misunderstand me, Lucifer dear," she whispered, her own eyes beginning to glow with an emerald gleam, "I already have immortality, brother mine. Daddy gave it to me for my last birthday. He wanted to do something to make up for stranding me in this Hell-forsaken place."

"Huh?" He pulled back to look at her more closely. "Desdemona...?"

She laughed. "It's been a long time since my last visit Below... I must say, you've grown quite a bit." She reached up to caress him teasingly and continued, "I will admit... the idea of eternity by your side does have its appeal. 'Better to reign in Hell,' right?"

Lucifer grinned, the sodium arc lights of the parking lot glinting off sharp, sharp teeth. "They do say that, don't they? It might be worth a try..."

"Mmmm... maybe you're right. Daddy's been sitting on that obsidian throne for more millennia than any one being has a right to... Certainly couldn't hurt to give it a go, could it?" She lay back and opened her arms invitingly. "Ready for some fun?"

"I think it's going to be one Hell of a night," he grinned, lowering himself into her waiting embrace.

The Alliance of Absconders

David Turnbull

The hooded tillerman steered his course, the black barge cutting a steady channel between bloated corpses that rolled on foaming rapids. Every now and then dozens of these corpses would resurrect, gasp for breath and try desperately to flail for the jagged shore. The undercurrents were strong. They'd be dragged under, the only reward for their effort to drown again, revive and drown again.

The sky was forked with lightning. A deluge of blood tainted rain bounced from the deck. Naked and shivering, Pascal cowered with the others, wailing with them in consternation, wondering in which circle of Hell his soul would be compelled to alight, his tattooed, bullish neck pulsing with anxiety.

The bloodied rain created an oily slick on the deck, causing them to slither around as the barge was tossed on the rapids. Like dodgems on some nightmare fairground ride, they'd slam into each other, only to spin and skid away.

This was how he came to crack skulls with Khalid.

"I know you," said Khalid, vigorously rubbing the wound on his head with one hand, while gripping Pascal's blood greased shoulder with the other. "You were involved in that robbery. You were holding those people hostage in that café. I

97

saw your face flash up on the news around about the time I was overdosing."

Pascal felt the blood from his own head wound trickle down into his left eye. He grabbed Khalid's lower arm to prevent them from being separated if the barge was thrown into another lurch. More than anything a conversation was what he needed to afford him relief from the horrors all around him.

"Did the cops get you then?" asked Khalid.

"Obviously," said Pascal. "I felt six bullet go in. Then darkness fell."

"Khalid," said Khalid, shaking Pascal's hand.

"Pascal," said Pascal in return.

"Our souls are damned," said Khalid. "I was a drug dealer. Too fond of my own product for my own good. I floated away on an illicit chemical high. You shot that security guard."

"He wasn't supposed to be there," said Pascal defensively.

"You shot him," said Khalid. "And now you are a murderer. Damned like the rest of us."

Pascal regarded him. Skinny, ribs showing on his chest, straggly black hair, goatee beard, mid-twenties at push, probably a good fifteen years younger than him. A complete contrast to Pascal's own weather beaten features and scarred physique.

The others, pathetically scattered like basking seals across the deck, began to wail. Pascal felt a cry rise like bile in his throat. It was almost irresistible. Khalid forcefully pressed a red stained finger to his lip. The cry receded.

"We need to keep our wits about us, brother," he said, fixing him with an intense stare from his dark brown eyes.

"For what?" asked Pascal, still holding on tightly to Khalid's thin wrist. "We're damned. What wits do we need now all hope is lost?"

"There's always hope, brother," insisted Khalid.

Blood rain bounced from Pascal's shaven scalp. White water crashed against the side of the barge. It lurched to the left. Still holding on to each other, they spun across to the other side of the deck, crashing painfully into some of the others in their wild, enforced trajectory. Pascal felt his spine jar as they slammed into the raised side of the deck.

"We have no hope," he groaned through gritted teeth.

"We can try to escape," said Khalid.

Another fork of lightning raked the sky. Thunder juddered through the hull. The hooded tillerman did not flinch as he steered his course.

"Are you mad?" said Pascal. "Escape to where?"

"Back along the river," said Khalid. "To its source. To reality. To life."

The wailing rose to a crescendo again.

Pascal blinked blood out of his eyes. "We're in mouth of the abyss," he said. "Descending to the inferno. We can't outrun the Devil."

"We can try, brother," said Khalid. "Guys like us were born running. Why should we stop now?"

"And how would we get off this barge?" asked Pascal. "We'd drown like those poor bastards out there if we dive overboard."

"I have a keen eye, brother," said Khalid. "Whenever there's a bend in the river, the tillerman steers close to the bank. That's our window of opportunity."

What the hell, thought Pascal. The kid is right. I grew up in the arse end of Brussels, fighting all the way for every scrap. Why should I stop now?

"What have we got to lose

Khalid grinned a white toothed grin. "Exactly, brother."

The barge bounced on the rapids and sent them careening across the blood soaked deck.

**

The concept of time slipped away from Pascal but Khalid didn't. Somehow they managed to hold on to each other, despite the relentless rain and frequent, agonising collisions with their fellow passengers. It might have been an hour; it might have been a day before they spied the course the river curved in a wide arc to the left.

The tillerman's clawed hand jerked the tiller. The barge sliced through the pink rain tainted foam of the rapids, nudging tumbling cadavers with its prow. They drew parallel with the shoreline, where Pascal could make out a flat, muddy expanse littered with what seemed to be white stones and boulders. It looked like a good place to run.

"Get ready, brother," said Khalid.

Pascal nodded and let go of the skinny arm, desperately hoping the barge would not be buffeted into another sudden lurch. The two men climbed up onto the side and crouched, ready to jump. Beneath the cowl of his hood the tillerman appeared too focused on his piloting duties to notice

"Now!" yelled Khalid.

They made their leap but fell short of the bank, splashing thigh deep into the rain lashed water. It was uncomfortably hot. How scalding it might be toward the middle of the river didn't bear thinking about. The discomfort spurred them both in a mad dash for the bank.

The barge passed around the arc of the bend.

Without a word they set off at a brusque jog in the opposite direction.

What had seemed like boulders and stones from the deck turned out to be bones lodged deep in the mud. Thigh bones and shoulder bones, coiled spinal cord, tibias and rib cages. And skulls: hundreds and thousands of rain drenched, red stained skulls, stretching far to the crimson horizon. Off in the distance a lightning bolt struck one of these, scattering shattered fragments.

Another barge turned in to take the bend, steered by another hooded tillerman. Yet another was following behind. The decks of both were filled with naked, wailing men and women. On the far side of the river a barge was on its return journey, empty of its pitiful cargo, heading no doubt for more.

"The world is brim full of sinners," observed Khalid.

From behind them there came a series of ear piercing howls that chilled Pascal to his core. He looked back. Far along the bank three dark objects were bounding rapidly in their direction.

"They've set the hounds on us," he said. The roof of his mouth turned dry with dread.

"Guess we're not the only wise asses to ever think of escaping," said Khalid.

No wonder the tillerman wasn't too perturbed by our departure, though Pascal.

"Let's head for the rocks." He pointed to a mottled outcropping jutting out into the river. "Get ourselves on higher ground."

He broke into a sprint, racing head down. Khalid was only a fraction behind, managing to keep pace despite his diminutive stature. The hounds howled again, causing the hairs to stand up on his spine. The red rain beat again his scalp. The sky above boiled and roared and spat lightning.

He hit the rocks in his stride. They were wet and slimy and impossible to climb without slipping and falling. He dropped to all fours and began an awkward crawling ascent. Khalid followed his lead. When Pascal glanced back he saw the three dark hounds, huge and hellish, coming across the mud flats, leaping the protruding bones like demonic horses in a steeple chase.

He slither forward and wedged his feet and hands into cracks and crevices. The air reeked of decay, mingled with a strong hint of something else. Something musky and vaguely familiar. The rounded surface of the rock he was traversing juddered and moved. He realised with a sickening certainty that these were not rocks but human bodies. Legions of them, interlinked and intertwined in into a huge peninsula of festering flesh.

And they were alive. A living hive of the damned. He could hear sounds coming from deep within the mound - moans and groans and sighs. And he knew exactly what the underlying smell was. It was the smell of sex. This wasn't just a pile of living corpses, it was an orgy of the dead. Pascal regarded the film of slime coated his hand and felt abject horror. There was more than a slight possibility that there was ejaculation and bodily fluids infused with the bloody run off from the rain.

He had no time to ponder because Khalid scrambled frantically past him.

"Faster, brother," he yelled. "Climb faster!"

Pascal looked back and saw that the trinity of unholy hounds had reached the foot of the mound. Snarling with terrifying ferocity they were tearing at the corpses with their claws and chewing out chunks of flaccid flesh to gain footholds and for their pursuit. He pushed himself forward and followed Khalid toward the peak of the mound.

Now that he was conscious of what was happening beneath him, he could feel the rhythmic synchronised lust filled molten that pulsed through the erotic assembly. He could feel the judders of completion and climax. The thrust of crotches. The arching of backs. He could hear the orgasmic sighs and cries.

He forced back his repulsion and chased Khalid's desperate scramble.

103

His progress was abruptly halted by something clamping tight around his ankle. He turned to see a blue veined hand had seized him, jagged broken nails penetrating his skin. He tried to kick himself free. Another hand took his wrist in a vicelike grip. An arm came snaking up and curled round his back to his waist like a python. Ahead of him, he saw Khalid had been equally incapacitated. He managed to twist his neck and saw the hounds tearing and clawing their way ever closer.

A face emerged in the space between Pascal and Khalid, pushing its way up past thighs and hips and buttocks. A woman's face, black in complexion, tainted with green putrid streaks.

"Join us," she beseeched. "Fornicate, copulate, and masturbate. Indulge fellatio and cunnilingus."

The head sprang upright to reveal a shock of dreadlocks woven with multi-coloured strands or wool. "Join us," she urged again, blue veins streaking the whites of her eyes. "Join us in endless orgasm and ecstasy. Cum and cum again. In unity there is strength."

The fierce growling of the hounds was growing closer.

Pascal struggled to free himself but more hands had him now.

"Let me go," Khalid was yelling. "Let me go, you damned perverts"

Now Pascal felt new and dreadful sensations. Cold kisses from cold lips. Soft nibbling of dead teeth. Caress of flaccid flesh. Slowly but surely he was be pulled down into the belly of the mound.

This was the rock to the hard place. Horribly seduced and corrupted on the one hand. Torn to shreds on the other.

"Wait!' he yelled. "In unity there is strength. An injury to one is an injury to all."

"What?" said the woman, her head jerking in his direction.

"Look what those mongrels are doing to some of your number," he urged her.

A pair of arms pushed down on the sensually writhing corpses. Shoulders and naked breasts appeared beneath the dreadlocked head. Black flesh streaked with the same green taint as the face. When she saw what the hounds were doing to gain purchase her eyes went wide. She let out a screeching roar of outrage.

Pascal felt the hands that were pulling him down loosen and let go. The copulating bodies of the mound tumbled into a mighty avalanche bearing down on the braying hounds. As the mound rolled forward, Pascal and Khalid rolled backwards, falling like swimmers behind the crest of a breaking wave. The hounds yelped and whimpered as they were crushed to bags of bones.

Pascal was the first to his feet.

He grabbed Khalid by his straggly hair and hauled him upright.

The two men hit the ground running.

***

They ran even faster than they had before.

105

Ahead of them lay another flat expanse of mud, littered with protruding bones. A barge passed along the river, the desolate keening of its passengers echoing to the shore. The blood rain continued its relentless downpour, never easing for one second. The sky rumbled and spat electrical forks. To his side Pascal could see Khalid was flagging, breathing heavily, shoulders slumped.

"You need to rest, friend!"

"Do you remember how long we were on that barge?" asked Khalid.

"I vaguely remember a tunnel. Long and dark," replied Pascal. "I thought it was a dream. Then the wailing started and I was brought to my knees by the absolute clarity of where I'd ended up."

Khalid came to a halt, hands on his knees as he coughed and wheezed. "I remember the tunnel," he said. "We have to get there. But how far, brother?"

Pascal shrugged his shoulders, looking nervously back to see if any more hounds were on their trail. All he saw was the mound settling back onto itself and throbbing in an unsettlingly lustful rhythm.

Khalid cleared his throat and spat on the ground. "The real curse of this place is that you can still feel pain and fatigue, even though you are apparently dead."

There came a loud explosion which shook the ground. When Pascal looked in the direction the sound had come from, he saw a plume of dark smoke rising into the red mist of rain.

"Someone else trying to escape?" he wondered out loud.

"Blasting through the tunnel?" asked Khalid.

"Got your breath back?" asked Pascal.

Another explosion sent a judder through the ground.

They wove their way through the skulls and bones and ran toward it.

***

They found themselves not the mouth of a tunnel, but on the fringes of a huge battlefield. Two armies of ten thousand or more men and women faced each other with all the weaponry humankind had devised through the ages to afflict pain and death on themselves, from ancient spears to missile launchers. Some of the combatants were dressed in modern day combat uniforms, others in mediaeval armour, yet others in naught but hide and furs.

Pascal and Khalid fell cautiously down onto their bellies and watched in wide eyed awe as row upon of opposing soldiers fell dead beneath showers of arrows and rapid fire rifle volleys. Limbs and torsos were being torn apart and tossed skyward by grenade and mortar explosions. Here and there they could see hand to hand, close quarter combat; bayonets lunging into bellies, broadswords hacking of hands from wrists, tomahawks splitting skulls.

"How do we get past this?" asked Pascal.

"We wait till the last man falls," said Khalid.

Pascal turned to him, a quizzical look etching his face.

"Who know what massacres and atrocities these soldier were guilty of?" said Khalid. "My

107

guess is that this is the forever war. These poor souls are condemned to battle it out into infinity. Like the bodies in the river, they die and revive and die again. When it all falls momentarily still that will be our window of opportunity."

Pascal winked at him. "You and your window's opportunity."

Khalid grinned back.

"We'll have to run like the clappers before the shooting starts again," said Pascal.

"We should take the opportunity to steal some clothing," said Khalid.

"And some weapons," added Pascal.

The battle raged on until the last to face each other across an ocean of gore and mutilation was a Samurai and a Zulu warrior. The Samurai sent his katana spinning through the air at the exact same moment the Zulu launched his spear. The blade of the katana lodged in the Zulu's eye. The spear penetrated the Samurai's breast plate and pierced his heart.

Both fell dead.

The sky darkened and filled with a cacophony of voracious caws and wingbeats as a biblical plague of grotesque, oversized crows descended onto the battlefield to peck out eyes and draw tongues like worms between their beaks. Amongst them scurried tiny horned imps who burrowed into open wounds and emerged with entrails and muscle tissue dangling from serrated teeth.

"We need to move, brother," said Khalid, launching himself forward.

Pascal didn't need to be told twice. The nearest corpse he found was dressed in khaki camouflage gear and desert boots. Pascal shooed away the crow feeding on the cadaver, hurriedly dressed himself in the dead man's trousers, tunic and boots and then armed himself with his assault rifle.

Khalid appeared, lugging a battle axe, dressed only in a tartan kilt. He looked Pascal up and down. "Are you sure all of that won't slow you down, brother?" he asked.

Pascal considered how the tunic, sodden with blood rain, was probably twice its normal weight and how the rifle was awkwardly unwieldy and how the mud might cling to the tracks of the boots. He cast the rifle to the side, stripped to the waist and kicked off the boots. "You're pretty damn smart for a low life drug dealer," he said, testing the balance of a Roman short sword.

"I am pretty damn smart," countered Khalid. "Back in Algeria I was a straight A student. My father had wealth and influence. He sent me to Paris to study structural engineering. But he cut me off completely when he found out about my lifestyle and the habits I had developed. That's how I came to be a seller as well as a user."

Pascal narrowed his eyes. "So what was all the crap about the two of us running all our lives?"

"I was running to free myself from privilege," said Khalid. "You were running in the opposite direction. Our paths were bound to cross eventually."

109

"Well, we'd both better start running in the same direction pretty sharp," said Pascal, "before we get caught in the crossfire."

On the battlefield corpses were twitching into reanimation. The first shots were being fired. Skirmishes began to break out. Pascal and Khalid were hit by the gusting backdraft of beating wings as the crows and imps rose skyward.

***

In their headlong flight from the forever war, they came across a tribe of blind folk, aimlessly milling and wandering on a gentle incline which rose from the riverbank. These lost souls stared ahead with milky white eyes, skin stained red from the rain, arms outstretched before them like zombies in a Hollywood movie, no more apparent purpose than cattle in a field.

Those that ambled too close to the bank were snatched and roughly rolled into the steaming shallows by fierce creatures the size of prehistoric alligators. Pascal and Khalid moved cautiously higher up on the slope. Behind them came the sound of explosions and automatic gunfire as the battle raged on anew.

They ran, elbowing and shouldering any of the shuffling presbyopian corpses that lurched into their path. There was no day and no night in this place, just the rumbling churn of the sky, the crack-crack-crack of lightning, the beat-beat-beat of blood rain. Pascal felt exhausted but he knew that if he lay down he would not sleep. The damned were

110

allowed no respite. There was no rest for the wicked.

As they ran he reflected remorsefully on the sequence of events that had led to his soul being cast to damnation. A jewelry store in Marseilles. Planned to be a quick in and out job. Display lots of aggression, point loaded weapons at the staff, yell abuse at them. The threat of imminent violence enough to make them compliant. Enough to ensure no violence actually occurred.

But they hadn't counted on the guard being there to make a pick up. In their dash from their parked motorcycles, neither he nor his accomplice, Verlain, had clocked the security van at the corner. The guard stepped out from a back room. Without a word he fired and brought Verlain down with a bullet to the thigh.

He turned to Pascal. Pascal pulled the trigger on his pistol. His intent was to incapacitate him with a shoulder wound. But in that moment the guard crouched low to take aim. Pascal's bullet shattered his plastic visor. His head jerked violently back as the bullet entered at the bridge of his nose.

Pascal fled like a coward, leaving the guard for dead and Verlain bleeding out on the shop floor. The screams and yells of the staff stabbed at his ears. Outside the sirens of multiple police vehicles were approaching. Pascal ducked into a half empty café – and found himself in the fatal hostage situation he'd never intended.

Khalid grabbing suddenly at his elbow brought him abruptly brought him back to the moment. "Our way is blocked, brother."

111

Ahead of them, spreading down to the river at one end and far to the horizon in the other, was a vast thicket of dwarfish shrubs, boughs trembling and swaying in an agitated manner as the red rain lashed down on them.

Inevitably things were not as they first appeared. As they drew closer they could see that these odd looking *shrubs* were in fact human beings, rooted into the dirt from the waist down, covered in moss and sprouting fungus, so wizened and gnarled it was impossible to decipher either gender or race. Their mouths gaped wide. Their faces were contorted, as if they were screaming but making no sound at all. Their mouldering arms flailed wildly, grasping for an escape that would eternally elude them.

"I reckon there's only one way through," said Pascal, nodding at Khalid's battle ax.

Khalid considered the ax and swung it at the nearest torso. Its left arm spun through the air, creating the beginnings of a gap. Khalid pushed on, swinging the ax left and right, loping and pruning limbs to clear path. Pascal followed behind, cracking heads with the short sword to protect them both from snapping teeth.

They progress this way, like dogged jungle explorers, till Pascal noticed his companion's energy was beginning to deplete once more. His swipes lost their power. He had to hack at limbs twice or thrice to get them to drop. He was slipping frequently on the blood slicked ground.

Pascal placed a hand on his skinny shoulder. Khalid turned, drenched in sweat that dripped from his goatee. Pascal held up the short sword. "You want to swap round?" he asked. A look of relief washed over Khalid's face. He handed over the ax with unreserved enthusiasm.

With the benefit of Pascal's upper body strength their progress picked up pace. But time remained ponderous. The sky churned. The thunder rolled. The lightning forked. The blood rain lashed against their backs. The deeper they cut into the human thicket the deeper it seemed they would need to go.

Pascal hacked away a clearing and kicked the fallen limbs amongst the torsos. They took a breather in the midst of this writhing circle of silently screaming souls. Khalid sat down and wiped grey brain matter from his arms and kilt. Pascal sharpened the ax blade with a fragment of hip bone he'd levered from the dirt.

"There!" cried Khalid, jumping to his feet. "I saw something."

Pascal looked to where he was pointing. East to where the river ran. He could see nothing but the red mist of the rain. But when the lightning flashed he saw it in the moment of bright illumination. A huge white arch the size of the Arc de Triumph.

"The tunnel entrance," yelled Khalid.

They allowed themselves a moment of celebration, whooping and bumping fists. Then they set off. Lopping and slicing. Swiping and pruning.

***

They staggered at last to the arch.

113

Its wide curve was constructed from hundreds of skulls set in semi-circular rows, one on top of the other. Just above the tunnel entrance itself was a layered pattern of skeletal hands, overlapping on the left curve, with a similar pattern to the right. A left hand and right hand clasped where they converged. To either side of the tunnel six skeletons were standing on one another's shoulder so they looked from a distance like the bones of giants.

Barges were emerging from the tunnel entrance, decks filled with wailing passengers, hooded tillermen steering into the rapids. On the other side of the river empty barges were lined up prow to stern, ready to collect fresh cargo.

"I'm not going to attempt swimming," warned Pascal.

"We need to climb over the arch," said Khalid. "Those empty barges form a perfect walkway."

They secured their gore caked weapons in the waist bands of their trousers and kilt and began climbing, inserting fingers into eye and nostril sockets, feet balancing precariously on the teeth of lower jaws, progressing like monkeys over the archway, not daring to look down to the river below, both dragging every last ounce of energy they could muster for the climb as the blood rain cascaded over the skulls.

They scrambled down onto the opposite bank then leapt onto the empty deck of the first barge. Red rain water dripped from the high ceiling of the tunnel, echoing in staccato as it plop-plop-plopped into the river. They ran the barges, jumping from one to the next and not one of the hooded tillermen

114

made any effort to intervene and stop them. It seemed they served no other purpose than to pilot the barges.

In the distance Pascal could see a tiny pinprick of light. They were almost home and free. Hope swelled momentarily in his chest but it was short lived. Something was rising out of the oily waters. Something huge and monstrous.

Both Pascal and Khalid came to a halt as it emerged. It looked like a wolf, but a bizarre, aquatic version of a wolf. Fins for ears, scales instead of fur, gills pulsing on its muscular neck.

"Go no further," it growled at them.

They both adopted a defensive stance, weapons raised.

Before their eyes the creature transformed into something else. Something with horns and cloven hooves and fiery red eyes. The Earl of Hell. Satan himself. "I've indulged you too much," said the Prince of Darkness. "It amused me to watch your fruitless flight. But now it is time to get back on board a barge and accept your fate."

"We've come this far," said Khalid. "Why should we stop now?"

Pascal conceded that the expected thing to do in the presence of the personification of evil would be to tremble with fear and prostrate one's self But his friend was right. They'd come so far. Endured so much. No matter the cost, they had to keep going.

The Devil transformed again. Now he became a grotesque mimicry of Charlie Chaplin. Putrid flesh beneath a battered bowler hat. He walked on the water, twitching his mildewed moustache and twirling his cane as he glided towards them in splay footed eeriness.

"Go no further and I will make you both tillermen," he offered. "You can learn to navigate the river. A barge each. As such you would suffer no torture or deprivation."

"I've never been one to hold down a steady job," quipped Marcel.

"If you could stop us you wouldn't feel the need to offer a deal," Khalid pointed out.

Chaplin chuckled. "I could so easily have stopped you. There are all sorts of abominations I could have summoned. But I was curious to see how far you would get. No one has ever reached the tunnel before."

"I reckon that's what's gotten you riled up," said Pascal. "Any power you have stops at the mouth of the tunnel."

Chaplin's bloodshot eyes filled with rage. He snapped his cane petulantly in two and began to tremble and transform. This time the Devil took the form of a gargantuan multi-limbed creature, part arachnid, part spider, towering malevolently over them.

"There's nothing for you beyond this tunnel,' it roared in fury. "You're dead. Your souls have been cast into eternal damnation. Neither of you is Jesus fucking Christ. There will be no resurrection. No rolling of stones. Beyond this tunnel there is a mirror image of here. Your flight will simply be reversed and you'll end up back where you belong, on one of my barges!"

"Why should we believe you?" challenged Pascal, craning his neck. "You're the Devil. Lies and deception are your currency."

Without warning, six invisible bullets slammed into Pascal's torso. Thump-thump-thump. Thump-thump-thump, echoing the circumstance of his recent demise. Beside him Khalid giggled, swayed and stumbled, seized by a pre-overdose euphoria. Pascal fought back the urge to fall into a quivering heap, as he had on the steps of the café, Pascal straightened his back and pushed out his chest.

"It's not real,' he said to Khalid. "Smoke and mirrors."

Khalid shook his head and managed to regain his senses.

"Shall we take our chance, brother?' he asked, shoulder to shoulder with Pascal.

"What's to lose?" replied Pascal. "Damned if we do. Damned if we don't."

With a liberating roar they ran toward the promise of freedom, weapons swiping against the ferocious whipping of limbs.

All That Falls

Ken L. Jones

Miles Mahler never wanted to have a job like this but now he did. Several abortive years as a would-be novelist had reduced him to taking a position as a grade school janitor just to put food on the table. There was something more than unsettling about the school he had been assigned to and it had little to do with the fact that it was the oldest one in the vast school district that had hired him. It had been the first school in all of Anaheim and had been erected in pioneer days. The old school building was still there but had been remodeled back in the fifties to serve as its teachers' lounge. Miles hated the school from the beginning because he was expected to do about three times as much work as the other day janitors did at the many schools where he had substituted before being hired full-time here. The worst part of it was the trees. Real honest to God virgin forests didn't have as many trees as this place did and all of these shed leaves on a year round basis. In addition to all the other chores he was required to do, he was expected to rake up all these leaves and keep the grounds spotless. This proved to be an infinity type proposition and was impossible to accomplish. The old building principal, who was dying of lupus, wasn't very nice about it.

Even though it was against union rules, Miles early on figured that he was expected to come out to the school for free on Saturdays for several hours just so he could stay even with the never ending falling leaves.

It was on such a Fall Saturday, a cold brisk day, he first noticed that the school was haunted. He paused in the middle of raking a giant pile of leaves as he heard the familiar sound of several of the ancient classroom doors opening and then closing. He suspected vandals or thieves, so he took the heavy rake he held just in case he had to defend himself and hurried back to that part of the school. There was nothing and no one there. He returned to his raking but again experienced the phenomena several times and finally gave up responding to it because it was getting dark and his wife and children were expecting him home for dinner.

This, and similar things, occurred over the next several Saturdays he worked at the school. Each time he was there these anomalies seemed to increase in complexity and duration. Finally, on the tenth trip, he actually encountered somebody at what should have been an empty school campus. He was an elderly American Indian dressed in traditional garb. He had long white braided hair and, as Miles stared at him in wonder, he noticed that the old fellow's eyes were devoid of sight.

The old man spoke to him in a hoarse broken style of English. "Why you white man on this land? This burial ground for my people. Sacred place."

Miles didn't' know how to reply to that. He studied the old man and came to the conclusion that he must be some kind of medicine man, perhaps some kind of sorcerer of great power but before he could speak further with this strange old man, he began to shimmer and seemed to evaporate before Miles's eyes like a mirage.

This strange visitation troubled him all through the next working week and on Wednesday, when the district painting crew arrived to begin to paint the buildings, he told old Ted Tyler, the lead painter of the crew, what he had seen while he had been plying his extra duties the previous weekend. They were drinking coffee in the back of the giant painting van together and Ted seemed kind of amused at the whole thing. Normally this reaction would have upset Miles but he liked Tyler who, like him, was from the state of Iowa and who reminded him of his own recently deceased father and so Miles took it in his stride.

Tyler lit a cigarette and began to talk to him as a father would a son. "I'm not a bit amazed to hear this. I've been living in Anaheim since I mustered out of the Navy at the end of World War II and I've been painting this school every year or two ever since then so I've heard some things about it. One day, years ago, I was talking to the grandmother of one of the kids here while she was waiting to pick up her granddaughter. She was telling me she used to attend this site back when she was a little girl, when it was just a one room Little House On The Prairie type of affair and that strange things went on even back then. I definitely think there's some kind of Indian burial ground around here somewhere because about fifteen years ago a giant sinkhole opened up back near the lunch area and there were all kinds of Indian bones and relics found. I thought for sure some archeologist would want to come and start digging but that wasn't the case. They had us fill it in as fast as we could and then we blacked topped over the top of it too. So what you're telling me makes lots of sense. If I was you I'd be careful, especially when alone on the campus on the weekends."

None of this did anything to weaken the apprehension that Miles felt about the school and, as the week went on, just being there, even when there were several hundred other people with him, started to feel wrong and ominous as if something was lurking, waiting to pounce on him. Finally Saturday came again and he almost decided not to go to the school. He wouldn't have if his job wasn't hanging in the balance. Reluctantly he made his way to the last place on Earth he wanted to be that day.

Ten minutes into the leaf raking, the worst amount of high strangeness he had ever experienced on the old campus began. The whole place seemed to be alive and throbbing and he swore that he could hear the sound of moccasined feet hitting the earth as they danced, accompanied by the droning prayers of Indians who sounded mournful in their supplications. Finally deciding he could stand it no more, he began to return his rake and the trashcan on wheels to the custodial shed in the rear of the campus so he could leave when he again was stopped dead in his tracks by the specter of the old shaman.

"Enough! This go no further. Three days all this stop. You good man me think so you no be here then. Stay home with family and be safe."

Too startled by this to say anything very complicated, Miles just nodded and softly mouthed, "Thank you," then, white as a sheet, he staggered off to his car and somehow made it home.

He did not want to upset his wife as he had never shared anything about what went on at the school with her, so he pretended to have the flu and spent the rest of that day and Sunday in bed, trying to forget all that he had seen and experienced.

Monday came. The old principal was livid and said so in the scolding way that a parent sometimes uses to talk to a child and then he told him more firmly than that it better not happen again. This upset the young man almost as much as what was truly bothering him.

Although he tried to ignore the events of the previous weekend, he found that was impossible. Every shadow and creak on the ancient property made him jump a foot and the next day was even worse. He was so visibly shaken that people noticed and asked him what was wrong, including the old building principal who called him in for a lunch time conference. Not really meaning to, Miles blurted out what was eating him. His boss didn't even try to conceal how crazy he thought his new day janitor was. He picked up the phone at his desk, called the foreman of janitors and told him to send a substitute the next day, after informing him that Miles was having some kind of a personal problem that required him to be off for a while.

The next three hours dragged by like they were made of solid lead and then it was time to go home. Still not wanting to tell his wife the truth about all that had happened, Miles made up a story about how he had strained his back doing heavy lifting and so he wouldn't be going to work for the next few days.

He slept in the next morning and almost felt right with the world again until his wife rushed into the room and turned on the local news. There was a remote news broadcast from the school. Everyone on the scene was frantic like they had been on the day of the 9-11 bombings. As best he could piece it together, a massive wind had started early in the morning and about an hour after school started every leaf on every tree in the whole place had been blown off and covered the entire school. As impossible as it sounded, the school had drowned in leaves, every inch of it had vanished beneath them much like the old town of Pompeii had disappeared beneath the volcanic ash of Mount Vesuvius. Even more impossible than that was that nobody could escape from this remarkable mass and no one could gain entry into it either. Even more troubling than that was that no traditional method of rescue seemed to produce the desired results either. Several tractor blades had mangled in the attempt and even several jackhammers had their bits explode when they were deployed.

Through it all the horrible screams of the trapped children and the school personnel there with them never ceased. It was heart-rending to hear them say that they were running out of air as they pleaded with those outside this weirdness to rescue them. This went on for longer than anyone could stand and then was abruptly replaced by something worse than that: total and absolute silence. The unfolding of all this caught the world's attention and every second of it was broadcast on TV. Miles more than anyone else was riveted to it in his home.

Two days later, after everyone had given up on finding a conventional way of addressing this problem, something happened that was even stranger than any of this. A mighty wind came up and tore into the leaves which now seemed to be nothing more than they should be. They were carried off into the sky for parts unknown. The news personnel covering this event were speechless at what they beheld because now they could see it clearly there was not one trace of the large campus that had once been there nor were any of the people who should have been there ever found, alive or dead. In its place, incredibly, was an elaborate Indian burial ground and in the front of it, seated with his legs folded, was an ancient mummified old Indian shaman who, with a shudder, Miles recognized immediately as the specter who had warned him to stay home. All of this was too much for the young janitor to bear. The ancient shaman was right. What was theirs was theirs and no one would ever be able to properly explain all that had so tragically transpired and so he never even bothered to try.

From that day on the very sight of falling leaves caused Miles Mahler to turn pale and shake like he was one of them himself.

The Wild Side

Olivia Arieti

Douglas had a wild soul, unrestrained and rebellious that more than once caused him trouble. Since school was too limitative for his nature, he dropped out, left home and began living on promiscuous expedients that led him, still adolescent, into a rehab centre. The walls with their grim barbwire were sky high and assured a perennial stay. The fear of being stuck there for the rest of his days was so strong that, after severely wounding a nurse and a guard, he ran away.

He managed to hide for quite a few years before getting in trouble again. It was all Rhonda's fault, though. He fell for her because she was as wild as him, perhaps even more. Not to mention her beauty; the hair had stolen its blackness from woods of ebony, while the eyes had captured their greenness from the lush of the jungle. As savage as evil, she mastered her instinct with human acuteness and easily captured her prey.

A ranch lost in the prairies where they could unleash all their energy and live without restrictions was the best place to settle down. Taming the untamed, wild mustangs always on the run, had become their daily challenge and at night time they huddled in their huge brass bed where also wantonness knew no limits.

Rhonda's wilderness, though, was too much for him. Kindled by her bestial rapacity, he grew morbid and jealous, insanely possessive. Ironically, he couldn't let her free.

After finding out she had cheated on him, early one morning, he followed her to the bush and his blade pierced her heart like the fangs of a beast; then he ripped off her clothes and left the naked body to the vultures, the rightful end of whoever dared to be more untamed than himself.

This time he didn't get away with it although he never confessed. The prison walls looked higher than ever and escape was impossible. He shouted so loud that the cries echoed like horrid howls among the endless corridors disturbing the other prisoners' feeble peace or consuming torment, then he wept and pleaded, all in vain. Stuck in his little cell, Douglas felt buried alive and was sure he'd die like those who woke up in their coffins.

Slowly, acceptance replaced refusal and disobedience; the price was depression. Guilt and regret got hold of him too and, exhausted, he let apathy take over.

For sure, an infamous curse had been launched on him since a child.

The situation was so bad that he had to undergo medical treatment; when he recovered, the outdoor world didn't appear as appealing as before.

Also the sky looked less blue and the birds swapping their wings as though willing to stir his past emotions went unnoticed. He felt safe where he was and let his fever slowly burn out like a dying fire…

***

Douglas was much older when he trespassed the prison's gate. His first visit was to Cathy, the doctor who helped him out. She had aged too, but was still attractive; mild and sweet and the opposite of Rhonda. Much to his own surprise, he fell in love and nothing made him happier than marrying her and moving into her cosy cottage.

The years that followed were as quiet as to appear tedious, but he relished every moment.

Apparently, the curse had been broken.

Regrets only didn't abandon him and one night he woke his wife and muttered, "You have to know the truth, dear, *I* was Rhonda's murderer."

Cathy remained silent for a long while then she started crying. She sobbed for the rest of the night and the following day and the day after till her eyes were as red as her cheeks and the lips swollen with froth. On the third day, she suddenly smiled and prepared him a succulent breakfast. The episode was never mentioned again and both carried on as if no confession had been made. She only kept her bedside table's light on every night.

Douglas was relieved although the luminous streak disturbed his sleep. The remains of Rhonda's body, maybe still rotting somewhere out there, haunted his dreams that most often turned into gruesome nightmares.

Strangely, Cathy's death didn't grieve him much; shortly afterwards, the old feeling re-emerged and all repressed or buried emotions

127

tickled his spirit anew. He grew restless, impatient, tense.

His damned thirst for freedom had always been lurking somewhere inside him...

The cottage now looked awful with the white wooden fence circumscribing it. The rooms appeared small and the ceiling seemed to have lowered upon him. Also Cathy's little garden was detestable and, in a fit of frenzy, he chopped off all the roses, daisies and lilacs.

Rebel and daunting once again, he looked at the past years like lost.

Visits to the nearby pub became more and more frequent, likewise spending the nights roaming around. While drinking apparently, quenched his thirst, it also increased his instability and the dread of ending locked in again became obsessive.

By chance, Douglas met an old friend who was a survivalist; nothing more irresistible than treading the uncontaminated, the wild and facing the extreme; his excitement was at its utmost.

The forests way up north were the chosen area. A few days later, he was wandering there alone and free to let loose his renewed vigour.

The adventure though, lost its appeal quite soon. Food supplies were becoming scarce, the weather was most inclement and loneliness especially at night time, frightening.

He shuddered on seeing the reflection of his face in the little lake; a hoary old man with deep wrinkles, an uncouth beard and dull eyes stared back at him. Perhaps staying at home would have been better.

The memory of the cosy cottage made him smile... He also thought of Cathy, the only person he hadn't hurt unless his confession stabbed her more than the knife that had killed Rhonda.

In the infinite nights, Rhonda's image, too, flashed before him; surely she would have loved to share his latest experience with him. Too bad he destroyed her...

The wilderness surrounding him looked brutal, raw and although now totally uncontrolled, he felt trapped by its grandeur. The fear of wandering too far limited his steps, of starving his hunger and the menace of beast attacks threatened his sleep. Many were the inhuman cries, howls and wails resounding around; no sooner the sun had set than the forest began letting its voice be heard. It was terrifying. Not only beasts but also uncanny creatures dwelt there and were ready to devour him. The trees became bleak shadows and the night fowls winged demons ready to plummet down and plunge their claws into his skin.

The rustles of leaves made his turn round; a magnificent exemplar of wolf stood right in front of him. Its greyness sparkled as though dusted with frost, the eyes were aglow; it kept glaring at him surely pondering when to attack.

Mesmerised by the animal's fierce poignancy, Douglas was unable to move.

Neither was he frightened for in his sublimation of the wolf, he saw it like a supernatural being, almost divine, that never would have stained its fur with blood.

He wished he could touch it, hug it and envied its pure freedom, driven by instinct only.

Finally, the nature of his curse fell upon him like a horrid truth; the spirit and the heart of the beast were inside him, a nasty trick of nature that gave him a human shape and a feral soul.

The animal's mouth started watering in the anticipation of the fleshy dinner.

"I love you," Douglas whispered just before the wolf leapt on him and let its jaws do their job.

Sick Girl

S J Townend

Sick Girl lives in the city and works in the supermarket stacking shelves and sweeping floors. Sick Girl is really good at her job and always leaves things tidy and always leaves the little boxes of cereal and cans of beans facing the right way around and pulled up to the front so it's easier for the customers to find what they're looking for. Sick Girl still only gets minimum wage and occasionally harassed by her landlord even when she is only a day overdue with the rent. Sick Girl is your modern day Cinderella story except Sick Girl isn't looking for a prince. Sick Girl went all Sinead O'Connor, all Bad Britney and shaved her head with a razor blade back at secondary school and no one asked her why she did it, which was fine by Sick Girl. Sick Girl's A-okay by herself, thanks.

Sick Girl was raised by Uncle as Ma was on the Horse. Uncle said Horse was Ma's Bad Medicine.

Sick Girl never got any medicine. Sick Girl's uncle did his best until he was on the Horse too and then Sick Girl had to look after herself. She kept her shirt sleeves long, her finger nails short and unpainted so the germs couldn't get underneath, so she could check for zinc and calcium and vitamin A deficiency and anaemia and heart disease easily. Sick Girl didn't need long nails. She always kept her door key to the bedsit that she struggled to meet the rent on poking through the knuckle slits of her clenched fists when she walked home in the dark after stacking shelves and sweeping floors and directing people to the milk. *The milk is always in the same place,* Sick Girl thinks. It's always in the same fucking place: first aisle as you come in the shop, underneath the massive sign which says, 'Milk'.

Sick Girl keeps herself to herself, lives alone and has no family now. Sick Girl is quite content with her set-up; quite content indeed with the way things are. Sick Girl works hard all week so she can eat organic and drink organic and wash organic and buy the things she wants: minerals and multivitamins and a digital sphygmomanometer; heart-rate watch and glucose-urine sticks and a litre a week of hand gel. These are a few of her favourite things; the thing she needs to maintain good health.

Sick Girl finds her weekend day trips always make her feel a little better. Sick Girl packs the same bag each Friday evening: map, pad and pen, phone and charger, neck pillow and some trail mix in a tub with 'trail mix' written on the top. Sick Girl decides to leave her gown at home this weekend as it is getting a little colder now and winter is in the air and the gown is quite revealing and doesn't always cover up the bits that need covering up all the time. Sick Girl waits until the Saturday morning to blend herself a green smoothie and make an avocado and pine nut salad, nice and fresh, which goes into its tub, the top of which is labelled 'avocado and pine nut salad', before heading off for the weekend.

Sick Girl walks, she likes to exercise—She knows exercise is good for the heart. Sick Girl pretends she is following the clear signage whilst pretending to look at the map she printed out and laminated a long time ago in preparation and makes her way through the double doors and down the clinical corridor until she finds the room she's looking for, where she chooses the chair with the most padding in the seat. Sick Girl likes to sit by the window so she can look outside as well as inside and knows both views will be relaxing as she has been in this room before, but not for a couple of months. Sick Girl looks up at the strip lighting— one tube is on the blink so she searches for a feedback form to complain about the lighting and finds one by the glass window which she presumes is a sub-station Reception as there is desk and a switched off computer there but it is currently unstaffed. Sick Girl fills in the form to let the caretaking team know that the strip light needs repairing because she knows that flashing lights can trigger epilepsy in someone who has never even experienced an epileptic episode before in their entire life. Sick Girl posts the form into the box by the sub-station desk and takes her seat again and then looks around and counts eight other people, most of whom, except for one, are staring at their phones.

Sick Girl smiles at the woman opposite her who isn't looking at a phone and thinks the woman looks like a bit like what her mum would like now if she'd gotten off the Horse before it'd been too late and cost her all her teeth and some of her flesh. The lady opposite smiles back, pulls a crossword from her bag and stares at that instead. No-one wants to talk here. No-one is asking where the milk is and Sick Girl likes that. Sick Girl can smell disinfectant and cheap coffee and no-one is asking her to do or clean or stack or lick anything because there is nothing here to stack or lick or do or clean. Sick Girl sits and looks things up on her phone although the wi-fi is slow but faster than at her bedsit where there isn't any wi-fi. Sick Girl starts writing a list of words which excite her beginning with the letter 'P'— Palliative, Parasitology, Paregoric, Paroxysm, Pericarditis, Polychrest—until her pen runs out of ink and she thinks about asking the lady opposite if she could borrow her pen when she's finished her crossword but someone comes into the room where they're sitting and takes the lady away before she can pluck up the courage.

Sick Girl continues to add to her list on her phone as she downloads an app which is just like a notepad, only on a phone and she wishes she'd discovered this sooner, like when she'd been at the beginning of the alphabet fifteen pads of paper ago.

Sick Girl watches people come and go until she is the only one left in the waiting room and her phone list gets longer and longer until it's no longer quite as light outside and in fact now its brighter inside than it is outside. Sick Girl wonders if it's time to reach into her bag for her neck pillow or if her stomach might not be full enough after the salad and the smoothie—maybe she should nip to the onsite shop for something else to eat before having a wee rest?

Sick Girl feels so content and decides she can wait until morning for something else to eat so she delves for her travel pillow, although she's not planning on travelling anywhere.

Sick Girl sees someone coming down the corridor with a clipboard and opts to leave her pillow in her bag for just a little longer. Just a minute or two longer, until the someone has walked on through to wherever the someone is going, but the someone stands in front of her and smiles with just their mouth and asks Sick Girl if Sick Girl needs any help and which specialist is she waiting to see. Sick Girl was so calm until someone came, but now Sick Girl feels her heart racing up into her throat along with a bit of smoothie and says she is looking for Pathology and the someone screws their face up like they're stuck on a crossword clue that they can't for the life of them work out the answer to and someone takes a small step back and looks up at the strip light which is strobing and quite annoying and after some thought, directs Sick Girl down the corridor and tells her she needs to ask at the Main Reception Desk as she is sat in Urology which is not the right place at all. Then, the someone walks off toward wherever they were going and Sick Girl sighs and gathers up her belongings.

Sick Girl heads to the Main Reception Desk but walks straight past it and looks at her map for options and chooses Dermatology because it's a little closer and she hasn't been there for a while and she is feeling a little tired after all the waiting and the listing that she has been doing on her day off after a long week at work. Sick Girl turns left, then left again, then up three flights of stairs, and then through a set of double doors into a smaller waiting room than before with fewer seats and no people. Sick Girl undoes her bag and places her belongings neatly along the window sill which is just above her head and sits in the chair underneath it and the heating is on full blast. Sick Girl relaxes again until she sees a man in a wheelchair being wheeled in by a nurse who applies the brakes and leaves him at the other side of the room and Sick Girl tries not to make eye contact with him because for a moment she doesn't feel safe in the room, but he is wheeled away again very soon and once again, she is alone and safe. Sick Girl notices the strip lights are all working in this waiting room which she finds satisfying and she places her neck pillow behind her head and closes her eyes.

"Excuse me, madam," are the words that wake up Sick Girl and her lids lift straight away. She was only having a light nap—there is no sleepy dust in the corners of her eyes at all—but now it's pitch black outside and the strip lights feel harsh again even though they aren't the flashing sort.

"Excuse me. Sorry to wake you up, dear." The words are coming again. Sick Girl wipes her eyes and sits up straight and doesn't know what to say.

"Are you okay, duck?" More words. Sick Girl knows she needs to say something back as that's the way conversation operates and she has had training on it and she knows this from the weekdays, when people ask her, 'where is the milk?'

"Yes. I'm okay." Sick Girl can see that this someone is a nurse and she's standing in the doorway to the waiting room—or maybe she is a someone who works in admin who gets to dress a bit like a nurse but doesn't have to sit the exams or deal with bodily fluids.

"We're closing the department in a minute. The cleaners will be round shortly. Dermatology closes at 9pm. Are you waiting for a someone?"

"Um. No, not waiting for a someone," Sick Girl replies in truth, her heart is thrumming faster now and is all up in her mouth. "I think I might be in the wrong department."

"Well, may I see your Confirmation of Appointment letter and I can escort you to the correct department myself," says nursey, who's not even smiling with just her lips.

Sick Girl picks up her travel pillow and her smoothie bottle and her pad and her pen that has run out and her phone and her empty sandwich box and the copy of a health magazine she picked up (on her walk over from Urology that someone had left on a chair) and the handful of leaflets on Prostate Problems, on Dealing with Dialysis, on Uterine Prolapse and on Contact Dermatitis, and shoves them all in her bag before swinging her rucksack over her shoulder.

"No I don't have a letter," Sick Girl says, shrugging her shoulders and deciding to call it a day whilst checking her map even though she knows the place like the back of her hand. Sick Girl heads towards the exit.

Sick Girl returns to the place where she stores her clothes and sleeps. She pulls out the box of rusty sharps stashed underneath her bedside table, rolls up her sleeve and sets to work on the canvas of her skin. A crimson river drips down her arm. The pain that no doctor can remedy momentarily dissipates into the silence of her bedsit prison. Sick Girl Screams. Sick Girl feels free.

First published by PUNK NOIR MAGAZINE (2021)

Escape of the Egg Thief

Dan Allen

The chickens didn't terrify her, although they should have, with their cluck-clucking and their sharp little beaks and those horrible, clawed feet. Oh, yes, especially the feet, constantly scratching, shuffling, and kicking up dust. But Jazz felt quite comfortable amongst them and looked forward to her daily visit. Oleg, on the other hand, terrified her. His ruthless demands unnerved her as much as the locked doors and barbwire topped fencing.

Jazz dreamed of her chickens and the long walk through the tractor shed to get to the stairs. Here the air was stale, spoiled with the reek of old diesel fuel and the floor permanently stained carcinogenic black from decades of oil leaks. The shed was always too dark for shadows, it concealed many hazards and Jazz hesitated with each step. Pitchforks and shovels dangled from the walls and a rusty plough blocked the aisle. The chickens were tucked safely on the second floor to protect them from foxes and the still lingering radioactive dust. Apparently thirty-five years was still not nearly enough.

In her dream, Jazz was running. First, she had to get to the stairs. Next, she had to feed her babies, her squawking little collaborators.

Somehow she made it to the top and stood on a narrow plank magically suspended in the centre of a never-ending black void. Infinity stretched below and the henhouse door loomed in front. Jazz could smell the chickens, their pungent odour brought back the seductive sensation of pain. Jazz threw herself at the door, excited to be with her hens. But the door didn't open and she fell. Her arms flailed and she watched the door get smaller and smaller until it was only a tiny dot. Then, finally, Jazz landed on something soft and it was nothing like she feared. Except for an annoying buzzing in her ear, everything seemed fine. But it wasn't real.

She fought her way back from the depths of the dream, climbing up slick, moss-covered walls until the glow of consciousness kissed her forehead. A smile teased at the corners of her mouth and she woke refreshed. A trio of flies buzzed against her bedroom window in a futile effort to escape. A few of their dead comrades, belly up and dried to a crisp, littered the mantel. *What a messed up dream,* Jazz thought and threw aside the bed covers. A familiar smoker's cough rumbled from the other side of the house. *Light up another one, Oleg. It's just one more nail in your coffin.*

"Jazz, you up? Let's go, girl. Time to get working." Oleg barely got the words out before hacking up another lung.

Jazz buried her face in a pillow and silently screamed. Cinderella, Cinderella, mop the floor, do the dishes, hang the laundry... I can't take it anymore! Eat shit and die, you nasty pig-faced man.

"Move it now! You know better than to test me. I've never spared the rod raising you, girl, and I'm

140

not about to stop." Oleg cleared his throat, he sounded like an old farm truck trying to start.

Jazz sat up[again. Her welt-covered body was a constant reminder not to dilly dally. *Coat hangers, belts, wooden spoons; I wonder what it'll be today.* Oleg's favourite disciplinary tool appeared to be an old fabric store yardstick, a relic from a bygone era. It had the right amount of flex to leave a sting and Jazz was sure if she could only see her backside in the mirror, she'd find a history of scars going back to her childhood. *A living testament to my abusive confinement,* Jazz thought. *I should report him to the authorities, show them my bruises, have him locked up.* Jazz hesitated as she visualized a pair of handcuffs and shook her head. There were no authorities. No police or even neighbours to help. They lived in the restricted zone, west of Prypat and thirty kilometres from Chernobyl. *No, there is another way to be free and I'll get there soon.*

She dressed quickly in shorts and a tee-shirt and hurried toward the door. A passion called and she couldn't wait to get back to the loft.

"Be careful not to breathe in too much dust," Oleg warned. "You'll catch salmonella and I'm too busy to be anyone's nurse."

Dust? Dust my ass. Radioactive or not, everyone knows dust in a chicken coop is dried bird shit. It dances and swirls in the air, tickles the inside of your nostrils and saturates your skin. Jazz visualized herself sitting on Oleg's chest, pushing handfuls of chicken guano into the man's mouth. She smiled for the first time since waking. "Salmonella sandwich," she mumbled.

141

"What's that?"

"I said, save me a sandwich."

***

Jazz crept into the shed and moved along the wall, careful not to let her shorts get soiled from a brush against the tractor. Her yellow rubber boots were a bit too big, but the chickens seemed to be rattled by them and that was good. *I'll wear my sundress,* Jazz thought, *and my white sandals too.* The sundress had never been worn. Jazz found it in the attic and fantasized it belonged to her mother, a woman she never knew.

Something moved above her and the idea of white sandals faded into her subconscious. Jazz glanced at the old hand-hewn beams which supported the second floor and slowed her steps, allowing her eyes to adjust to the darkness. Crystal strands wove a labyrinth of silver, reflecting even the tiniest bit of light. A furry mass rested in the centre of this work of art. Orange and brown hair-covered legs protruded from an enormous golfball-sized abdomen.

"You're an ugly beast, aren't you? You stay away from me, mister."

Perhaps annoyed at Jazz's interruption, the spider scurried away and vanished into the rafters.

"Where did you go, you gross piece of puke? I liked it much better when I could see you." Jazz had a vision of the spider dropping from above and crawling through her hair. She shivered and hurried to the stairs.

142

The stairs had been salvaged from the remains of an even older shed and were a carpenter's nightmare. They were awkwardly steep, some sloped forward, others tilted to one side or the other. They were all spaced at random heights and the entire mess was better suited for a clown's funhouse. The rickety stairs rose straight up from the middle of the floor with no handrails or walls to lean on. Jazz took her time; her knees began to wobble by the third step. She crawled the rest of the way and only stood once she reached the top.

She pushed against the henhouse door. It had swollen over the years and now scraped against the floorboards, slowly digging a groove. The birds usually ignored her, but today an old grey hen took an interest. Perhaps irritated by recent events, the buzzard-like beast appeared hateful and made a ruckus... flapping and clacking and stirring up the other hens.

The chickens nested in a wall of boxes, stacked up like tiny condo apartments, each with a screen door to enable egg collecting. Behind, a brilliant series of ramps provided the hens access to their square foot of privacy. They laid one egg a day in a never-ending attempt to fill their nest and they seemed to enjoy the community lifestyle, all except for old Grey. She never took to crowds and Jazz made her a bed in a small drawer liberated from an old dresser. The drawer was about as wide as long and made a perfect nest once loaded with straw.

Jazz finished opening each little door and collecting the surprise inside. Now she only had the drawer in the corner to check and she felt anxiety crawling over her skin like newly hatched sand fleas. Grey's eyes were closed and Jazz gently felt around beneath her for the hard-shelled oval. The girl had become adept at this; her tiny hands and nimble young reflexes gave her an advantage.

Jazz's slender fingers touched the shell and she reached deeper to get the grip needed to ensure a swift extraction. The buzzard's left eye cracked open and Grey took a hard peck at the girl's arm. Jazz pulled back her right hand, avoiding the jab and reached in quickly with her left, stealing the egg before the hen could strike again. It was all a game to Jazz and a grin of satisfaction crossed her face.

"You tried to bite me, didn't you?" she asked, fully expecting the creature to answer her. "You're a bad bird."

Then Jazz made the mistake of turning her back and walking away. Grey hopped out of her box and, in one stealthy sprint, was close enough to take a shot at the girl's tender milky-white legs. Grey's raptor-like beak (powerful enough to split hard kernels of dried corn) opened wide and chomped down on a meaty section of Jazz's calf.

She tightened her fists and screamed. Then she turned and stared at the face of her attacker and waited for the pain to come. At first, it stung like a paper cut and Jazz closed her eyes.

The pain is good. It's part of the process, part of the plan; she reminded herself. Turn it to pleasure and learn to love it.

She concentrated and soothing endorphins rushed through her veins and flooded her body. She felt warm, her heart fluttered and beat faster and every nerve tingled.

Old Grey, either confused or indifferent, retreated to her drawer. The bird's biological clock kept ticking and in all likelihood, her body remained busy working on producing another egg.

Jazz slowly came down from her high and glanced at the small triangle-shaped cut in her skin. A slow-moving trickle of blood descended into her boot and she smiled.

***

Back at the farmhouse, she proudly presented her haul to Oleg.

"Take your boots off at the door, Jazz. You know better."

In her excitement, Jazz had forgotten one of the many rules. Now deflated, she sat on the floor and tried to pull her heel out of the rubber. The thrill of the morning collection quickly faded from her memory.

"You're bleeding. What did you do, take a fall?"

"Oh, it's just a scratch. I must have brushed against something in the shed. Unfortunately, it's too dark in there for me to see." Jazz lied, sort of, she wasn't sure why.

"Dark, humph," Oleg snorted. "Or perhaps you're just not careful enough. You've always been a clumsy oaf."

Later that night, when the house was dark and Oleg's snoring reverberated off the walls, Jazz sat on the toilet and looked at the cut under the bright bathroom lights. She poked her fingernail into the tiny wound, felt the pain and once again cooed with the accompanying rush. When finished, she stood in front of the bathroom mirror. The pupils in her bright blue eyes pulsed and she combed her shoulder-length golden hair. She felt good. So incredibly, amazingly, wonderful that she winked at herself before shutting off the light. The plan was brilliant and she shared her secret with the only person she trusted.

Jazz slept peacefully and was up before Oleg. She had the table set for breakfast and was pulling on those god-awful yellow rubber boots.

"My, my, look who's up already," Oleg said, still half-asleep without his morning coffee. An unlit cigarette dangled from his mouth and he tightened the strap on his ragged robe. "Are you feeling all right? You don't look so good to me."

"I feel wonderful! I can't wait to start my chores."

"Come here for a minute. Your eyes look glassy." Oleg felt her forehead, the age-old technique used to diagnose everything from a spring cold to the bubonic plague. "You're not hot. Are you stealing my vodka, Jazz?"

"No, not at all." Jazz felt a pang of guilt. Her drug was anticipation and pain.

Oleg grabbed Jazz's shoulder and squeezed.

"Jeezus, I said no." Jazz pulled away.

Oleg snorted and reached for a large wooden spoon.

Jazz flinched and the corners of Oleg's mouth curled. "I'm making oatmeal this morning and you know what happens if it gets cold." Oleg paused and tapped the spoon against his thigh. "It goes thick and lumpy."

Thick and lumpy like dog shit, Jazz thought and ran out the door, letting it slam behind her. Shw ignored the shadows and moved through the dark shed, skirting around a tractor and ducking under low-lying web strands. She raced up the steps and stumbled near the top, almost ending her day early. *Damn, that was close,* she thought and pushed on the door. It opened easier than usual. Perhaps her eagerness transformed into energy and boosted her strength.

The chickens were calm. Jazz would have thought this strange had it happened on any other occasion, but on this day, she paid no attention to their quiet wanderings and went straight to the condominium of nests. Most contained an egg, as they did every morning. *When Old Grey starts to lay less frequently, she'll find herself on the kitchen table.* Jazz thought about the idea of eating a roasted chicken dinner and shook her head.

"No. That's not going to happen to you, is it, my feathered nemesis? It will be you eating me."

As if understanding her words, Grey squawked.

Jazz bit her lower lip and reached for another egg.

Before she was through, a chill tickled the back of her neck. The room had become eerily silent, and

147

the air was heavy, almost like it was void of oxygen. Jazz looked over her shoulder and slowly turned to face a semi-circle of hens, all watching and waiting like disciplined sentinels. The birds were led by Grey and took a step forward in perfect synchronization as if they had stayed up all night practising. A row of ugly little heads bobbed and they took another step. They quivered and twitched as if the anticipation was too much for their small reptilian brain and it was clear to Jazz the hens would be unable to control themselves. Is this what she wanted? She had grown to love the pain. Deliciously wonderful in small doses. The hurt replaced Oleg's abuse and offered a strange, missing intimacy in her life. She had trained the hens, fed their appetite for blood and they were ready,

But I'm not ready, she thought. It's too soon.

Jazz didn't have time to reconsider for, as if released by a secret signal, the chickens attacked. Wings flapping and beaks snapping, they charged under the cover of a plume of feathers and aimed for her exposed skin. Instantly, small tidbits of flesh ripped free as if she were a loaf of bread covered in sesame seeds.

"Oh, yes! That's good, my babies. That feels so damn good."

This is the way it will be, Jazz thought, *when the day finally comes for me to escape Oleg's clutches and leave this hell behind.* Jazz tensed up and threw back her head. The chickens clucked and pecked and squawked, tearing at her soft young skin and spraying red droplets over the floor. *It's raining blood,* Jazz thought, but it didn't cause her alarm. Instead, she smiled, cooed and stood on tip-toes. She had never felt so alive. Her toes curled inside her rubber boots and she watched the flurry, like a feather kaleidoscope. All was well until Grey tried to peck out her eyes and then Jazz panicked. Attacking her face, her eyes… was too much and it frightened her.

"No! Stop it. Get the hell away from me!" Jazz swung wildly and the bird flapped and back-pedalled, always keeping just out of reach. Finally, as a last resort, the girl whipped the basket.

The damage could have been worse had Jazz not thrown the eggs, for the sight of broken yolks appeared to startle the chickens and they spread to the farthest corners of the room. Jazz stood in quiet wonder at the mess of her body and waited for the pain to return. When it came, she applied her trick. An explosion of pleasure washed over her body and she tossed back her hair and spread her arms as if she could see heaven through the dirty ceiling. *It feels like the taste of ice cream and cotton candy with the twist of a merry-go-round,* she said to herself.

Jazz had stopped them soon enough. Next time she doubted she would be able to resist. But that was okay. From the day she cut her hand and bled into the feedbag… from the moment she scattered the blood-stained feed, a plan had formed.

"I've done my best to train you and I feel you're ready. Oh, my beautiful little angels, you've tasted the forbidden fruit and now you'll set me free. I know you will."

Thirty minutes later, Jazz found herself back at the farmhouse. She felt flushed and perspired guilty pleasure. It was a pain Oleg couldn't give and a pain Oleg couldn't take away. Buried within this searing agony was the path to liberty.

Jazz left the basket of surviving eggs on the counter and disappeared into the bathroom before Oleg could see her damaged body. She cleaned herself up the best she could and used an entire roll of toilet paper in a futile attempt to bandage her legs. Jazz looked like a mummy for a brief moment until bright red spots blossomed and spoiled the illusion. She pulled on her favourite leggings and those too began to leak. Finally she squeezed into a pair of seldom worn blue jeans and snuck back to the kitchen.

Her oatmeal was cold and had congealed into something with the texture of clay. She ate it without complaining and hoped to make herself scarce before her captor could get a good look at her, but of course, she wasn't so lucky. Oleg came in from the fields and immediately went to the sink to wash his hands.

"For heaven's sake, girl, why are you wearing jeans on a hot day like this?" He grabbed a rag and patted the sweat on her face. "I thought my days of having to dress you were long over, but now... well, I guess I could pick out a few things." Oleg couldn't help but smile, apparently pleased with his subtle sarcasm.

"Maybe you were right this morning. I don't feel very well." Jazz used the excuse to hide in her room for the rest of the day. As long as she remained still, the blood clotted and the bleeding stopped.

Darkness had left the sky, but the sun was not yet over the horizon and the grass was still wet with dew when Jazz snuck out to the barn. She had learned to enjoy the pain the hens provided. It was the rest of her world which hurt. Jazz had trained the birds well. She would let them finish this time, let them end her suffering.

She had traded the jeans for a dress (the fancy one, saved just for this occasion) and her precious white sandals. She didn't bother to bring a basket. She wouldn't need it. But, unfortunately, Jazz's happy thoughts were interrupted by an angry voice she knew all too well.

"Where the hell do you think you're going in that dress!"

Jazz ignored her captor.

"You get back here right now."

"No," Jazz screamed. She had never been so defiant. Of course, the word "no" wasn't an acceptable answer, but this day was sacred, a graduation ceremony of sorts and she would not allow Oleg to interfere.

"You're going to pay for this, you little bitch. Oh, yes, you're going to pay for the rest of this year and next year and the year after." Oleg sputtered and mumbled.

The screen door slammed and Jazz risked a glance behind. Oleg was still dressed in his moth-eaten robe. He marched toward the barn, crushing the handle of the collecting basket as he went. His uncombed hair flew wildly about his face and he brushed it away with tobacco-stained fingers. He wore a pair of sheepskin slippers, the backs of which were squashed flat by his heels.

Jazz sped through the tractor shed and was partway up the stairs when a board creaked and moaned behind her. Thick, gnarly fingers dug into her shoulder and tossed her to the floor.

"You get your worthless ass back to the house. Hang up that dress and be waiting in the kitchen. Start a fire in the woodstove. We're going to have a special little talk." Oleg growled and pointed his finger. "Think of it as an opportunity to learn." Then he climbed the stairs to the henhouse door.

Jazz sat in a dishevelled mess and struggled to control her emotions. She imagined Oleg entering the room and the chickens attacking, gorging themselves on his fatty plump body. Old Grey plucked out Oleg's eyeballs and swallowed them whole. And finally, Jazz visualized Oleg falling face first and dying amongst chicken excrement.

Jazz's arms began to shake, and her body tremored. Finally, she hugged herself and fought off a tear.

No, Jazz thought. *The pain is mine. I can't let him steal it from me. I need to stop him. I need to be free.* Jazz sprinted after her captor, intending to relieve him of the egg collecting burden and the inevitable carnage which would follow.

Moments later, she paused inside the henhouse door. The room was silent and Jazz found she couldn't intervene, at least not yet. *Perhaps there is*

152

another way, she thought. *I'll miss the pain, but it might be just as much fun to watch.*

The chickens lined up like sentries along the walls and Oleg walked down the middle as if he were Moses parting the Red Sea. *It looks like he's running the gauntlet,* Jazz thought and then she looked for old Grey, hoping to see if she would take the first nibble. As if reading her mind, the bird appeared at the end of the receiving line and scratched the floor like a bull ready to charge. It was a signal for sure and, in an explosion of squawking feathers, the birds attacked.

"Please…" Jazz shouted, but her message was unclear. Did she mean *Please don't do this?* Or perhaps she gave them permission like *Please, yes, please! Kill the nasty old bastard.* Jazz wasn't sure and it was too late to back out.

It didn't seem to matter to the chickens. Beaks and claws worked in a frenzy and shredded the man's flabby body. Jazz watched, unable to control her enthusiasm. By merely observing, she felt the pain, the glorious cleansing pain and she squeezed her legs together. Old Grey took a peck at Oleg's chubby pink cheek and pulled off a small piece of flesh. The others noticed, flapped around his head, pulled on his shoulders and they eventually dragged him to his knees. Small fragments of his scalp, each with a few strands of white hair, floated like dead dandelions in a breeze. A bird hovered, frantically flapping its wings to remain in place and drove a gnarled foot into Oleg's mouth. The sharp claw pierced through his lower lip and ripped it in half. Perhaps from memory, Jazz tasted the blood, thick like warm cooking oil, and spat out a ball of phlegm. Unfortunately, Oleg didn't have the same option. His wiggling tongue made too good a target and it was soon removed. Two chickens fought over the pink treasure until a third swooped in and bit off more than her share.

Jazz watched to the end. Speckles of blood decorated the walls and the floor looked as if someone had installed a crimson shag carpet. The birds continued their rampage and left nothing identifiable apart from a pair of sheepskin slippers, ripped pieces of robe and a tarnished Chernobyl Survivor medal. Jazz's sundress was spoiled forever, covered in a bizarre pattern of blood-splatter polka dots. Her white sandals, stained red, were also ruined.

Old Grey picked up the medal and carried it to her box. Jazz took off her sandals and put them gently beside the nest.

"Here, have these, too, if you're collecting souvenirs. You've been a good adversary, Old Grey. I was willing to die for freedom, but thanks to you, I don't have to now."

Grey squawked and flapped her wings as if she somehow understood. Jazz reached down to stroke Grey's head and the bird took a chunk out of her thumb.

Thatta girl, Grey. Thatta girl. Jazz thought, then headed for the stairs. Kyiv was a hundred kilometres to the south and she looked forward to the walk.

A Darker Shade of Freedom

Rie Sheridan Rose

She drifted through the party, saying hello to friends and acquaintances as she passed. She felt like a princess in the dress of silver tissue lamé. It was something she could never have afforded for herself, but was pleased to take advantage of.

"There you are, my dear," murmured Jordan, putting an arm around her waist and dropping a kiss on her cheek. "I was beginning to think I'd missed you."

She steeled herself not to flinch at the touch. "I'm sorry, Jordan. I was seeing to our guests."

"Always the considerate hostess." His eyes were hooded as he studied her.

She feared there was something behind the light words. Had she done something to displease him? If so, there would be pain before sunrise.

Offering a nervous smile, she asked, "Is there something you needed from me, Jordan?"

"Just your company, my dear." His hand tightened painfully around her upper arm, crushing the delicate fabric and making her wince. "Come with me, if you would."

Yes, there would be pain.

She allowed herself to be led away, knowing it would be worse if she hesitated or struggled. It was a familiar scenario. Almost daily. He was very good at creating bruises where they were least noticeable.

But if she accepted her punishment quietly, there were fewer of them.

She trailed after him like an obedient dog, hating herself for doing it.

How had she come to this? She had been carefree once. A college student with a goal of becoming a teacher. And then she'd gone to a party with a friend who had introduced her to the suave, urbane Jordan—a rich, handsome erudite man who had fascinated her beyond belief. They had struck up a conversation that lasted well into the wee hours of the morning... and she had been hooked. He had reeled her in with flattery and gifts, sweet talk and tender kisses. But once she was caught, everything had changed.

Now, even the slightest mistake could have dire consequences. She'd learned to keep her mouth shut and her eyes open. She was the one who flattered and submitted to his every whim. She was nearly at the breaking point. One small push might be enough to send her reeling over the edge into madness.

Funny, that. He'd reeled her in and now he was reeling her out.

Jordan practically dragged her through the house once they were out of sight of their guests. What transgression had she committed now?

"Look at this pig sty!" he roared, shoving her through the bedroom door.

She glanced around the room wearily. She'd been taking a nap before the party and the bedclothes were a little mussed. The closet door was open an inch or two. Her slippers were beside the dressing table instead of the bed. Other than that, the room was the magazine-spread perfection he insisted on.

She stifled a sigh and moved to pick up her slippers.

Quick as a snake striking, Jordan grabbed her hair and slammed her head into the marble top of the vanity. "How many times do I have to tell you?" he growled as her world went black.

***

She opened her eyes slowly. The air was hot and stale around her. She tried to sit up but her head connected sharply with a hard object. A raised hand felt above her prone body and found a solid surface as far as she could reach. She kicked her feet and determined that there were only inches around her in any direction. She couldn't shift it at all, even shoving with all her might against the surface above her head,.

She closed her eyes again. Her heart sank. She was trapped. There was no way out. Jordan had finally gone too far.

A single tear slipped past her control... and she realized there was an up-side to the whole affair. She might be entombed alive, but that would soon pass. A smile curved her lips.

She could stand a few moments of discomfort and pain to know that she would never again be subjected to the terror of Jordan. She was free at last.

Adrift

Jason R Frei

After a total of seven hundred forty-five days, Jill Warner finally tasted freedom. She supposed it tasted like ice cream or cake or pie, none of which she had been allowed to experience. There was much of the world that she had not experienced.

At fifteen, she was underweight by thirty pounds. Her brown hair hung down to her waist, twisted and dreaded from years of neglect. Her eyes and teeth sunk into her emaciated skull giving her the appearance of a death's head. Skin so white it was almost translucent stretched across her torso, showing off the knobs and spines of her bones. Her legs were so thin and frail that they barely held her body up.

For slightly more than two years, Jill lived, if you can call it that, against her will with Lester Aaron Gafney, the mortician and director of the Gafney and Sons funeral home. To everyone's knowledge, Lester did not have any sons, which might have explained his behavior. He was in the middle of a service when little Loretta Colton wandered into the back of the mortuary and discovered the four foot wide Goliath coffin where Jill was forced to live. She knocked on the side of the gigantic coffin and ran back into the parlor screaming when something knocked back.

158

Rather than risk capture, Lester pulled out a gun and shot himself in the head, sending little Loretta into hysterics as droplets of blood ran down her pretty dress. During questioning, Jill told a tale of being kidnapped by Lester when she was twelve years old. He kept her locked in the over-sized coffin, releasing her only to eat and to use the bathroom. At night, he laid his hefty, imposing body next to hers in the coffin. His fingers were delicate and nimble, but never once did they play on her body like they did on the church organ every Sunday. At least she was spared that horror, whispered the crowds.

***

Five years later, Jill sat in a waiting room, waiting for her turn. She traded her long, ratty hair for a short pixie cut, dyed pink and light blue. She held a Highlights magazine, running through a popsicle-shaped maze using her index finger. Every few seconds, her gaze flitted to the door, willing it to open. She debated getting the box of crayons and coloring in a dinosaur when the door opened and Dr Eric Strouse stepped out. His dark blue suit hung loosely on his pencil-thin frame.

"Good morning, Jill." His voice was soft and gentle. "Come on in."

He held the door for her and she passed by him, averting her body slightly so as not to touch him. She wasn't afraid of him, it was a habit she couldn't shake. She dropped cross-legged into the abundant leather, shivering slightly when it reminded her of

159

sitting in the coffin. Again, another reflexive action she couldn't shake.

Strouse sat in a cream-colored wingback chair. A yellow legal pad rested on his lap. His eyes were kind and they scanned her face. He noted the puffy, dark areas under her eyes and the way those same eyes darted back and forth, taking in the entire room. He knew she was looking for exits and preparing her emergency contingency plan for whatever might happen in the room, whether it was a difficult conversation or the zombie apocalypse.

He smiled slightly. "How are you sleeping?"

Jill snorted. "Same as always."

"And the nightmares?"

Her eyes shifted. "None this week."

He knew she was lying. Jill suffered from the same nightmare, played over and over in her head each night. She found herself in the dark, surrounded by impenetrable walls. She felt closed in, but at the same time, she floundered in open space with nothing to ground her. The darkness swallowed up her screams as soon as they left her mouth. When she finally accepted her fate of being alone in the dark, a large beefy arm wrapped around her from behind. Then, and only then, would she awake, her breath caught in her lungs, threatening to smother her.

"I can't help you if you aren't honest with me or yourself."

Jill scowled and then threw up her hands. "Fine! I've had it every night."

Strouse nodded. "What made that so difficult for you?"

The girl folded her arms sharply across her chest. Anger flashed over her face as she stared through the doctor. Her breathing sounded forcefully through her nostrils. After a moment, she dropped her head and stared at her knees.

"It's been five years and I don't feel like I've gotten any better."

The doctor sat quietly, waiting for her to continue.

"I can still feel his arm around me. Every night when I crawl into bed. Every morning when I wake up screaming. Even when I'm sitting in this chair." She looked up at the doctor, her eyes glistening.

"And do you know what the weirdest part is? The feeling of his arm around me is comforting."

A sob hitched in her chest and disgust blanketed her face.

Strouse wrote a few sentences on his legal pad. "Tell me about that—the comfort."

Jill swallowed. Her tongue clicked against the roof of her mouth.

"Have you ever been in a coffin, Doc?"

He shook his head.

"You'd think it would be tight, constrictive, like suffocating. But I was only thirteen and it was such a large coffin."

She closed her eyes and put her arms out like a T. Her fingers curled into fists.

"Lying on my back, I could reach each side with my fists." She opened her eyes. "It was massive. I was alone, for hours, in such a vast space."

"So even though you hated Lester and what he did to you, that arm was the only thing keeping you rooted."

"I hated Lester, but I loved that arm. It made me feel safe... secure. That's not normal, Doc."

"Normalcy is only relevant to the situation you are in. Fire can burn us, but also keep us warm. Guns can be used to kill people, but they can also keep us safe. The arm was just a tool. You can love the tool *and* hate the person using it."

"Is it normal to feel alone, even when I'm in a crowd? Or to need absolute darkness and confinement when I'm sleeping?"

Strouse sat forward in his chair. "You were in an abnormal situation, so the things you do because of that are normal for you. No one experiences trauma the same way, therefore, no one responds the same way." He paused to let it sink in.

"You said a little bit ago that you don't feel like you've gotten better. What would make you feel better?"

Jill let out the breath she had been holding and slapped the backs of her hands down on her thighs.

"To not feel like this!"

The doctor held out a hand. "Describe... this."

She sighed. "After everything he did to me—taking me away from my family, my friends, my life—I should hate him. I *should* hate him. Even you said so."

"But you don't." The doctor said this matter-of-factly, not as a question.

"I don't. I actually miss having that arm around me, keeping me safe."

Strouse pushed her on. "And why is that?"

"Because as much of a monster as he was, he took care of me. He didn't hurt me, at least not physically. He kept me fed. He let me out of the coffin from time to time. He protected me and gave me structure. He loved me unconditionally."

The doctor sat back in his chair. "And you don't have that anymore."

Jill shook her head. "No, I don't. I mean, I'm thankful for my parents. I can't imagine what they went through when I was gone, but they aren't the same anymore."

"Neither are you."

Jill nodded. "That's why I moved out, but I just feel kind of.. .lost. I thought I'd feel differently by now."

A soft chime sounded in the room. Strouse checked his watch.

"It looks like we're done for the day, but I think you did some great work. I want you to think about something for next week. Think about the safety you felt, the structure you had when you are with Lester. I want you to examine your life right now and identify some things you have that might help you feel that way again. Think about what you can control in the present."

Jill unfolded from the chair and left the room.

A young girl sat in the waiting room with her mother. She held the same Highlights magazine Jill had earlier. The girl looked up and their eyes locked for a brief moment. Jill smiled. It was in that moment that she realized what she needed.

***

Loretta Colton left school after serving her detention. She had about a mile walk home, but she trudged along wishing it would take longer. She hated home. Ever since she found that girl in the funeral home five years ago, her life had been flipped upside down. She was always in trouble at school and she couldn't focus on getting any of her work done. Her parents yelled at her all the time, or even worse, sometimes they treated her like she didn't even exist.

She was plagued by nightmares every night. The suicide of Lester Aaron Gafney played over and over in her dreams every night. Most of them were in shades of black and gray and white right up until the end. Then, bright splashes of red pervaded her vision until it was the only color left. The only sounds in her dreams were the muffled knocking of young knuckles on wood, right before Lester shot himself.

Worst of all was the fact that she had no idea what happened to that other girl. She remembered staring at her through tears as the kidnapped girl was escorted out. She looked like a skeleton in a stained white frock only slightly darker than her pale white skin.

Loretta was told many times that she saved the girl, that if she had not wandered off, the girl might still be there. Her parents said they were proud of her. Police shook her hands and took pictures with her. The news reporters called her courageous and a hero. What struck Loretta though was the look on the other girl's face when she climbed into the ambulance. She turned around once and her eyes found Loretta's, eyes that did not show relief and gratitude, but rather fear and contempt. Those eyes showed up in her dreams, right before everything went red and she woke up.

She was lost in her thoughts when she passed by the playground. She wasn't sure what caught her attention, the body lying face down in the sand pit or the feeble cries for help. She immediately went to her pocket for her phone, but it had been taken away when she told her parents about the detention. She hesitated briefly, looking around her and then ran to the prone body.

Loretta noticed instantly that it was a young woman. Her clothes were torn and dirty. Pink and blue hair stood out in stark relief to the dark gray sand. She bent down to shake the woman when the body flipped over and jammed a moist cloth into her mouth. Loretta gagged at the bitter taste. She resisted for only a few moments before falling unconscious.

***

She awoke in total darkness. Her head swam and nausea bubbled up from her stomach. She tried to sit up and almost immediately hit her head against something solid. Bright colors flashed and pain felt like it tore her skull in half. In a panic, she thrust her arms out to the sides and both came into contact with barriers. She thrashed back and forth.

165

Her screams sounded muffled and dead. She screamed until her throat was raw.

**

For three days, Loretta languished in darkened solitude. Her voice was gone. Her fists hurt from punching against her surroundings. She evacuated her bowels and bladder causing a rank odor to permeate her nasal passages. Her face crusted over from tears and snot.

On the third day, a latch creaked open and blinding light stabbed at her eyes. She was pulled roughly from her confines and a coarse, dark bag thrust over her head. Cords bound her wrists and ankles. She was dragged by her ankles across a bumpy floor and dumped into freezing cold water. It took her breath away as hands held her forcefully in the water. She tried to scream, but there was nothing left in her.

She felt her tender skin scrubbed with harsh chemicals and an even harsher wash cloth. The hands that did this to her though were not harsh. They were tender and delicate.

When the washing was complete, she felt herself wrapped up tightly in a large, soft blanket and deposited on a cool, tiled floor. Footsteps receded and a door was closed and locked. She was too tired to fight and laid there, only half conscious.

A short time later the footsteps returned. This time she was carried instead of dragged. The arms that held her were gentle. She whimpered only once when she was laid down. Her binds were cut and the sack removed from her head, but the light was still glaring. Until it went out and she was once again shut up in the darkness.

She reached her arms out and felt the familiar obstacles surrounding her, but also found a water bottle and a wrapper of crackers. She devoured them in mere moments.

**

This same ritual was enacted several more times. Loretta lost track of time and found herself losing a grip on her surroundings and herself. She imagined herself floating in space, like a satellite with no guidance. Space was cold and lonely. Oh, so lonely.

And then one day, it wasn't. She awoke to the normal darkness, but there was someone lying with her. A gentle and tender arm wrapped around her stomach. A warm body spooned around her. Instead of fear, she was grateful for the warmth and the security. She felt grounded and for the first time since this entire ordeal started, she smiled and breathed easily.

That night, she found out exactly what happened to the girl she rescued so many years ago. This time, she was the one being rescued. She felt free in spite of the cramped quarters. Loretta and Jill both found what they had been lacking these past five years—someone who understood what it was like to be them.

She Sells Seashells

Liam Spinage

I often saw her plying her wares. She would walk along the seafront, as bright and breezy as the weather and the weekend crowds drawn down from the capital by the new railway.

Until, one day, I didn't.

There were rumours she had succumbed to an illness, though as the town's foremost physician I found this remarkably hard to believe. The partaking of regular sea air and seawater had been a well-recognised tonic here since the days of Dr. Russell's patent medicines.

Her wheelbarrow still stood on the promenade, though it was starkly empty of wares. I wondered what might have caused her to abandon it. While I feared for her safety, others feared for my sanity, I had stopped promenading and started patrolling. I stopped passers-by and, armed only with a frayed photograph, began asking questions.

"Excuse me, have you seen this girl?"

The answer was most often a firm shake of the head accompanied by an associated melancholy which seemed to ask me a question back:

"Why this one? With the tide of humanity ebbing and flowing from the capital to the beaches and back, what was particular about this one person?"

Sometimes that was asked of me and sometimes I asked it of myself. I continued my practice, dispensing proprietary medicines of the sort Russell would have been proud of. Occasionally, when I ventured to the shore for more seawater, I lingered overlong and stared out, standing at that sacred time between the day and the night at that sacred place between the land and the sea. I had made a good living from it; I didn't deny that. I took those precious life-giving waters and used them to make a real change in the world. Yet there was always something fearful about those waters even when they were placid. When they were full of fury, they might devour the whole town without a second thought.

I looked back to those fishing boats still moored at the hard scrabble above the high tide mark and something struck me.

They would know.

I'd spent so much time asking tourists that I'd neglected those who knew too well how fickle a mistress the sea might be and here they were, huddled around a little fire on the beach to keep warm. Time has not been kind to our ever-dwindling fleet, the wind and water had not been kind to their pock-marked and weather-beaten faces. Still, I was familiar to them after a fashion and was in sore need of company who might understand.

There was a shift in their temperament as I approached them. I thought for a moment there might be violence. My mind shuddered at the fate of our seashell seller and whether they had a part in it.

Was I about to talk to friend or foe? There seemed no way to find out but to ask.

The fisherfolk were fortified with concoctions stronger than I had ever prepared and many of them were reeling drunk. Still, they listened to my impassioned entreaties and let me finish before they replied.

"Aye, we know her." One stood, a man rougher and older than his companions. Grey flecked his beard; rum flecked his lips. He seemed unsteady on his feet though I daresay I would be equally unsteady bobbing up and down in his little fishing boat. "Tho' we ain't seen her in these parts for near a month. Strange little thing... She kept 'erself to 'erself, took no boat but ne'er came back on an evening with aught less than a full haul. Many's a time we wondered where her spot was, but she never did tell. No, sir, she never did tell. Reckon as she'll come back?"

I replied in the negative and between us we allowed ourselves a moment which we both spent avoiding the impropriety of shedding a tear. I thanked them for their time and their honesty, I withdrew and made my way back along the beach, lost in thought as the stones crunched beneath my feet and the waves lapped softly in the distance.

At that juncture, I heard her voice calling. I swear till this day it was her voice I heard, so help me God, and I'll never forget the words she spoke.

"I can't take any more."

I whirled round, stumbling a little - I thoroughly admit this was out of fright and in no part due to the modicum of rum of which I had recently partaken - and tried to find a place for that melody of melancholy.

Nothing.

My senses reeling now from more than liquor, I tried to still the rapid beating of my heart.

"I can't take any more."

Again, that plaintive cry. Again, I tried to find the source and could only conclude it came from the ocean itself. I stepped forward with more bravado than I would have credited myself. I must know the answer to this mystery. Heavens, she might be injured! Was this the cry of a maiden in distress? Or the last gasp of a desperate suicide?

Before I knew it, I stood at the very edge of the water, waves breaking around my feet, and called out her name.

Silence.

I tried again. What I heard call back frightens me still to this day.

"And neither can you."

A great wave washed over me, drenching me in more brine than I sold in a week. I ran – away from the ocean, away from the beach, back to the safety of the town.

That voice was not hers. I would never hear her voice again; I know that now, unless I succumbed to the same call which had taken her.

The ocean knows.

It knows who has taken from it and it exacts a price for that taking. A reckoning of sorts. It giveth forth, but it also taketh away.

The following morning, I hung a 'closed' sign over the door of my business and took the railway to the capital. Never again would I set foot on the shore.

The Divine Masculine

Rickey Rivers Jr

I'm on the road heading toward the pier. I'm going there to meet my soon to be ex. He wanted to meet me there. I wanted him to wait. I know why he wants to meet me. He wants to break up. He wants to break up because his parents are getting divorced. I know what you're thinking: "What does that have to do with you?" That's the same thing I said.

The idea of a relationship at fifteen never made sense, but Calvin and I seem to congeal around each other. We managed to last five years before his feet went cold like an ice cream pop. Life is a mistake in the rear-view.

Looking forward now and I see him off in the distance. He's so far away that I don't see him with my physical eyes. I see him with my invisible one. I got into tarot readings.

"Someone in your present will soon be your past."

That's what the reading said and hey, who am I to defy spirit? I just never knew it would happen like this. One can't question fate. Fate will kick you right in the mouth, bend down and say, "told you so."

***

I met Calvin while both of us were still in school. Calvin was leaving the corner store as I was walking by. We caught each other's eye. I kept walking but Calvin caught up to me and we started talking. We talked so much we nearly reached my house before he stopped and remembered his house was in the opposite direction. We exchange numbers. The rest is history.

The past and future can be similar in the present. In the present you can confuse the two. If you're not careful your head will spin backwards trying to remember what you wanted to forget, or likewise trying to forget what you wanted to remember. I remember being in a terrible state of mind and wanting direction in life. That's where spirit came in, tarot saved me. I got away from my parental conditioning. I became free through the readings. I was able to find my particular life path in the cards. Those cards have helped me greatly. They've helped my relationship with Calvin, at least so far. For some reason over the last few weeks the cards have told me different tales. They've told me that the man would leave me. They've told me to be careful.

You see, tarot shouldn't rule your life, but you should think of spirit as guidance and spirit has guided me greatly. I'm so happy I've found a way to fully express the heart of hearts inside the heart of tarot. Nonbelievers don't register. I've been laughed at before. Even Calvin didn't believe or take heed until his life was also affected. You never doubt spirit. Sure, you can be confused, but to doubt spirit is a fool's errand.

There's no need to speak on parental guidance further. Everyone has something they dislike about their upbringing and mine wasn't anything special. I love my parents. I don't have many problems with them. It's Calvin who's got the problems. His parents have been constantly a problem. It's not my fault that his father cheats. It's not my fault that his mother drinks. And yet, who gets the blame? The loyal girlfriend.

It's not like I haven't been tempted to cheat, or drown my sorrows in a drug, but I chose not to. I chose to be better than my boyfriend's parents. But what does that get me at the end of the day? Broken up with, told that "this is too much for me right now." As if we can't work it out. Imagine not wanting to work with your girlfriend based off your parental situation. I don't care what kind of people his parents are. I care about Calvin and it hurts me that he can't see that I'm more than willing to work with him. He's the only guy for me, the only one I want. What's the use in living if you have to live without the person you love?

The day I met Calvin I felt something inside. I'm not talking childhood thoughts of love. I mean I truly felt a spark that lit the buried fuse. Before Calvin I was sick, constantly sick. I was sick of school and sick of life. Before Calvin I wanted to be one of those guys who got a bunch of guns and ran into the school to shoot whoever came into view. I know that's dramatic, but that's how I was. I was fifteen and lost; fifteen and sick. The world was one big zit combined with the zits on my face. All of

175

that made me hate the idea of living. It didn't make sense to be alive and suffering at the same time. Why not be dead and done with it all?

I don't often talk about these things with other people because other people don't seem to understand. I know what you're thinking: get therapy. Been there, done that, got the psych evaluation too. Guess what? Still here and now I feel the sickness return due to the breakup. That's right, the breakup, which technically hasn't happened yet, which technically I'm still on the road approaching. I could easily decide to turn around or drive elsewhere. So why am I running toward this future of further pain and sickness? I think it's because I know when enough is enough and when another person has had enough. I guess Calvin is just done with everything, done with me and his parents, or just done with me. That's fine. He should have just killed himself. That would have been easier. With that I'd understand. But wanting to get away from your girlfriend and using the excuse of your parental situation is completely unacceptable.

I know I sound angry, but I'm really not. I've accepted the idea and the problem. All of it is just whatever. Who cares at the end of the day? Why should I cry over spilled milk, or spilled Calvin?

Life can take you on so many different roads. Sometimes it's hard to turn back. You know who helped me learn to drive? Dad. You know who helped me when Dad got too nervous? Calvin. I love Dad, but he couldn't keep me calm on the road. Calvin was different, he knew the right words.

"Everything's fine."

"You're doing okay."

Actual encouragement is a great thing. Every teenager should hear it. Every teenager should know that someone is actually proud of them. Maybe then they wouldn't shoot up schools so much.

I remember reading about the last couple of guys who had fun like that. They made sure the doors were sealed beforehand then they got in through the window close to a cafeteria. A lot of schools are made so the windows don't open all the way, but you can still easily break them. That's the thing about schools; many are designed to resemble prisons. So you can't really wonder why the children are so much like inmates. Of course they are; nobody's sane.

Children often bounce off the walls from an adolescent on up. Can you blame them? Look at some of the environments these people come from. Not to say my neighborhood was peachy keen, but it's much better than some of the slums my classmates came from. And who wouldn't want to shoot up the school thinking about going to those prisons every day? It's not like the gunshots would be foreign to the inmates or foreign to the foreigners even. I know how all of this sounds. I'm not dumb. Remember, this is who I used to be. In the present I'm headed towards Calvin. In the present I'm crying with the sun in my eyes. In the present my tears are glistening.

I think I'm different from a lot of people because I'm not afraid to tell the truth. A lot of people hate the truth. They'd like to bury it in the backyard somewhere. But the truth can actually set you free. I know that's a corny saying but it's nonetheless true. I've realized this over time. A lot of people are just afraid in life, and hey, it's okay to be afraid. I'm afraid of some stuff, but the truth is never in the book of fear.

The book of fear contains exactly what it says on the cover. And I'm not trying to be mysterious or allude to some Lovecraftian mythos. I'm just speaking honestly from the heart. I believe we all have a book of fear within us, just like we all have a book of anxieties and a book of happiness. It's important to keep up with these books and write down everything relevant.

One of my fears is abandonment. I'm sure you've guessed that already. Abandonment is a terrible thing. I wouldn't wish it on anyone. And I know what you're thinking next: "but you had two parents." As if workaholic parents pay attention to their offspring. As I've said before, I love them, but at the same time, aren't we groomed to love our parents?

***

Love is something one shouldn't say unless they fully mean it. I'd never say I loved another person if I didn't mean it. So why would anyone say that to me? A person's heart shouldn't be played with like a toy and yet people will squeeze and squeeze until nothing is left of your vital organ but a pulp. I remember Calvin crying to me and

178

expressing all of his stress like I wasn't going to be there to help. Apparently that was the goal, for me to not be there, for me not to help. I remember wanting to grab and squeeze his vital organ. But those were the feelings of then. And the feelings of then must not permeate the present. We must always look to the future and the future is a breakup, a terrible thing. It'll be my first time.

I don't think you have to guess another first I've experienced with Calvin. The day was shortly after prom, the place was a hotel room. Calvin rented the room. It was on the outskirts of town. From there we could walk right to the beach if we wanted. But on that day we didn't want to walk. We just wanted to have each other.

Sex is combining with another person, congealing fully to become a single organism. What a pleasure it was to join together in stickiness with the person you were to marry.

Marriage, that's the word, that's what I thought. But why and how could marriage happen when your boyfriend can't sort out his parental situation? I've asked spirit. The answer is the same every time: it can't, it won't. It's simply impossible to join with a chaos person and Calvin is a chaos person. He can't even control his household. I know he lives with his parents like I live with mine, but my parents don't invade my privacy trying to force their life into mine.

As far as I know Mom and Dad still get along and even if they didn't, I wouldn't fashion my life after them. So why is Calvin fashioning his life after

179

his feuding parents? The cards have told me: it's not love.

It can't be love because he wants to end it. And if you end what you have with a lover, your only lover, how then can you want peace? You can't, you must want chaos.

***

I'm off the road now, I'm on the beach. I'm still driving. I see the pier. I see Calvin, with both physical eyes in the physical world. I feel the bumpy planks of wood beneath the tires. Then I don't see Calvin. I feel the car ram into a coward. And I'm still driving. I'm crying. I'm smiling. There's the ocean.

It's A Long Way To Sometime

Dorothy Davies

One step. One step me. Earth shook. Shook much, dust fell on head. My head. Dust on head. One step I took more. Dust fell. Do not want dust on head.

Two steps I do. Clever. I walk. Them said "he never walk." Them wrong. I walk. See three steps. Now no care about dust.

I want.

I want same as others.

Mother. Father. Brother. Sister. Home.

I want.

They not want me.

Four steps. Five steps. I walk. I walk good.

This. This door. This stop me walk any more. *Bang*. No door stop me walk any more.

This is. What they say? New.

This is. Room. Big. Walk here good. More steps. How many more steps. Ten more steps. I walk good. Them say "he never walk." Them wrong. I walk. I walk good. I no care about dust. I walk.

Oh. Person stop me walk. *Bang*. Person no stop me walk. No one stop me walk. I walk good.

I walk out of here.

I not like here. I not like noise. No. Not noise. Person sound. Scream. Yes. Scream. Person see me

181

and scream. I not like. I stop scream. *Bang*. Scream stop.

More person. More person run and scream. Say "he walk!" I say, "I walk good!" but I only make noise. Not word. Why I not make word? I big. I walk good. I talk – talk? Make word is talk? Person go from me. Good. I not like person. Stop me walk. No one stop me walk.

Out. Out door. Door no bang. Door open. Person – *bang*. Person lie down. Person not move. Good. No stop me walk. No stop me, I walk good.

What is light. Light in sky. Light is hot. Light is hot on me. I know I hair. Lot of hair. Person say, "he lot of hair." Good or not good? Person not say. I not know.

I walk. I walk good. Person scream loud and I go *bang* and stop person scream. Person run away. All person run away. I walk good with no person.

Dust fall on head. Earth shake when I walk. I walk good. I no like dust but I like outside. I like no person stop me.

Oh. What is – box. Round things. Noise. Scream. No, not scream. Shout. Shout STOP! *Bang*. Box go flat. Round things go flat. No more STOP.

I remember.

I remember Mother. Mother soft. No *bang* for Mother. Mother good. I remember Father. Father not soft. *Bang* for Father. Father bad. I remember brother. Brother soft. Small. No *bang* for brother. Brother run fast, cry, run, not me. I walk good. I no run. I walk and go – fast. Big legs. Person said "he has big legs. He take long steps." Other person said, "he no walk." Person wrong. I walk good. I take long steps. I go fast.

I remember sister. Sister soft. No *bang* for sister. Sister cry and – touch me. Touch hair. Call me "teddy bear." What is "teddy bear"?

I remember. Mother said; "I come and see you sometime."

Father no say nothing. Father *bang* lie down no move.

Brother say, "It's a long way."

I say "What is? Sometime?" I walk. I walk good. I walk fast. I see person run scream hide I see no person to *bang* no person to stop no person to bring box and round things to stop walk.

I go.

I go find Mother. I tired of room. I tired of bars. I tired of person who call me an – im – al and hit me. I *bang* person. I big. I strong. I bigger now. Mother know me.

I say, "it sometime. I come."

Brother say, "it's a long way."

I say, "it's a long way to sometime". No know what is but sound good in head.

No one stop me.

I walk good.

No person to *bang*.

Sometime. I come.

This is possibly one of the scariest stories I've written and, because of the influence, it is dedicated to the memory of Richard Burton Matheson (February 20, 1926– June 23, 2013) with thanks for the horror he gave us.

Train Screams

Joseph Genius

Us neighborhood children in Suffolk County all knew about the "screaming train ghost". A lonely old man laid down on the Long Island railroad tracks in the middle of nowhere, suicide by train. Or maybe it was a double-suicide by two young lovers. Nobody seemed to know exactly how it started but that didn't stop us from scaring each other when we rode the train. Ghost(s?) on the train track, crawling up the railroad car, hunting you.

I had long forgotten about it, but many years later when I was accepted to New York University, my commute meant taking the train to and from school. When it reached the long curve in the track, I heard the "screams" of the train which, of course, were really just the brakes and the wheels and the rails, all squealing together. I'd become so familiar with the sound that I barely even noticed it anymore.

One day, during the long morning commute, I fell asleep. I heard screams in my dream, but they were not from wheels or brakes or other train machinery. I looked out the window and saw what was making the noise; a twisted face of agony, screaming at me.

I woke, trembling with fear, still hearing the echoes of the screams that had pierced my soul. I turned to my window, half expecting a ghost, but

184

saw nothing but the grassy field and the old track-
side workers' shed in the middle of nowhere. Dream
or not, I had felt something out there and it terrified
me. I pressed against the window, peering out,
knowing this view wasn't good enough. I had to be
physically outside the train.

The next day I arrived an hour early at the
railway station, but I didn't get on the train. Instead,
I walked away from the station along the tracks,
convincing myself that nothing scary ever happens
in the daytime. Of course I didn't believe in ghosts
anyway, but I still wouldn't be here at night. I
walked the tracks for about thirty minutes until I
reached that middle of nowhere. I stood in a grassy
field, across the shed, I didn't hear any screaming or
much of anything, I looked around, waiting for the
next train to reach the curve.

Even before I saw the train I felt it, rumbling in
the ground. And that's when the screaming started.
The train was fast approaching but I was *already
hearing screams.* I froze. As the train passed it took
the screams with it and then there was stillness and
silence again. I remained motionless as I replayed
the screaming in my mind. It was not the train. I
looked up and down the tracks: there was nothing.

Then I looked at the shed about 30 feet away. I
had a decision to make; turn around and walk back
to the station, or walk the 30 feet and investigate. I
reminded myself, again, that screaming ghosts, or
any other kind of ghosts, don't exist. I walked
towards the shed, my legs less than steady.

When I got closer it was just as I suspected, a

normal old woodwork shed, one window, blackened by years of what I guessed was train brake dust. I noticed the grass was tall all around it, including the front door, which made it appear neglected or even abandoned. The door was secured with a thick, rusted chain and massively imposing padlock.

Well, I'd come this far. I tugged on the padlock, rattling the chains. The screaming started again from inside the shed and I immediately jumped back. The screams continued, freezing the blood in my veins. With a trembling hand I picked up a rock, smashed the window and was hit with a smell so foul that it shook me even more than the screams. That's when I ran.

That was last year. Yesterday, Anna contacted me for the first time, thanking me for discovering her and informing the authorities so they could rescue her. She'd been abducted as a child, kept alive only to be used by her captor. Chained for a decade inside that dark, rotting shed with nothing but the sound of the train and her screams.

In Search of Caliph Oneiroi

Liam A Spinage

Although this journal fragment is understood to document the fate of the lost 1929 expedition of Professor Flaubert, the provenance of this text cannot be verified by Miskatonic library staff. Those tests that have been carried out have confirmed that it is indeed penned with modern ink on thick papyrus. There is no entry for it in our cataloguing system, to the considerable vexation of our archivists Frey and Henley. All we can do is present the intact text below and allow the reader to draw their own conclusions.

We proceeded west from Cairo along a well-used trail into the desert - at night, naturally, since to begin such a journey under the glaring light of the Egyptian sun would have been sheer folly. Naturally, there were those who claimed our trip was folly anyway - a doomed expedition in search of a doomed caliph.

The night-blooming desert plants emitted a pungent, almost palpable aura which permeated the air around us. Only the chill of the night breezes kept our senses from reeling as our camel train vanished over the horizon from the city, far into the western dunes.

It was not long, I seem to recall, before our minds began playing tricks on us. We had been warned by our native guides to be alert to the mirage - that distortion and disruption of visual acuity which caused one to hallucinate through the heat haze. Pressing on through the day was not advisable in the least; indeed we had been countenanced against such an action several times in Cairo but I was adamant that our destination would be found in one of these deserted desert valleys and that it would yield its location willingly. What utter madness! What sheer foolhardiness! I know that now - and much more besides - and wish that I would have known it then.

When the day was nearly spent, we spied a light shimmering in the distance and instantly dismissed it as one of those self-same mirages which had plagued us under the harsh sun. Directionless and with our sight dimming in the darkness, we decided to head for it anyway; the only point of light save the stars on a sand-strewn ocean of utter darkness.

We approached the apparition which only grew in strength; its very existence was indeed firmly rooted in our reality. A lone bell tolled from the gatepost; echoing eerily even given the distance yet to cross and beckoning, beckoning, with its discordant yet somehow somnolent tones. Our heads grew heavy as we drew near and it was then we first spied the strange figure waiting for us in the doorway of what appeared to be the palace of a local potentate, somehow incongruously situated here in the deep desert. Was this indeed much wanted respite for a needy traveller? Or some fresh hell perpetrated on our senses? I considered these options as I surveyed the wonders of the courtyard. It was indeed a lovely place, lonely but welcoming in its way; as was the countenance of the young lady who greeted us. With a coy smile, she lit a single candle which burned brightly in the umbral gloom and beckoned us in, indicating that there was plenty of space inside for us to rest.

The corridor from the courtyard to the interior was lined with ancient statues fashioned to resemble the gods of the pantheon of ancient Egypt which had first captured my imagination as a small boy. I looked at each of their shadowed forms in wonder as we proceeded to what I took as a lobby. As I did so, I reeled in shock as the whispered winds through their stately forms carried words which, in hindsight, we should have known to be warning.

"Welcome," they seemed to say. I knew it to be problematic in the highest order for those words to be uttered in the mother tongue of old London, but I remained fascinated, unwilling and obstinate, not willing to give up what might be a vital - as well as excellent - place to take in water and sustenance for any further ventures into the inhospitable landscape which surrounded us.

"You will always find welcome here." I could no longer tell if the voice was emanating from those ancient Pharaonic forms which adorned the lobby or whether they issued from the lips of our erstwhile hostess. As she ushered us, exhausted and limp from our travails, through the lobby to an inner courtyard, I was struck by the impossibility that not only were there other guests but that each of them was a veritable symbol of virility; Nubian warriors conjured forth from the depths of time each of their semi-naked forms rippling with musculature from headdress to golden loincloth. Each of them was seemingly lost in a trance, undulating away to piped music bidden from the recesses of their own minds, glistening with sweat even in the depths of night.

Parched as I was, I inquired what refreshment might be had; all other considerations of this mysterious and forbidding place could wait until my addled pate had been restored by refreshing liquid sustenance which we had rigorously rationed during our trip. It was evident from her reply that such blessed waters were not currently available and I had to avail myself of the remainder of my own water skin just to keep my thinking clear as I was shown to the most sumptuous bedroom I have encountered outside of the hotels of Bohemia. Even as I slept, the voices continued to plague me. Had I heeded their warning earlier, I might have come fully to my senses and torched the place for the den of madness and iniquity it was, but alas! this was not the case.

I awoke, somewhat refreshed after a disturbing night's sleep, but famished. Since no staff saw fit to disturb my quarters, I dressed and began to pace the rich, carpeted halls of the palace, idly wandering through room after room, all jewelled and filigree beyond the ransom of a king, but empty, so empty. Mirrors adorned the ceilings, distorted reflections of my haggard form staring back at me with wasting, wanting eyes, locked in a horror of their own remembrance of better days. It then occurred to me to check on the camels, but I was unable to find the exit to the lobby. Each room distorted dimensions to such an extent that I, and those other admirable companions who had accompanied the expedition and since joined me in my increasingly desperate meanderings through this golden nightmare, were utterly, dejectedly lost.

Our exploration continued at a frenzied pace, keen to avoid the gazes of our mirrored forms bearing down upon us and fearing for our sanity, knowing that we were now likely prisoners here of our own folly and guilelessness. We finally came - by design it seemed - to a chamber that was different from the others, in which sat all of those nubile Nubian men we had seen the night before, swaying gently in cacophonous prayers which tugged the cords of our now-frail mental faculties. At the centre of this circle sat a bearded figure richly dressed in satins and silks with a large tome resting on his ample lap. Here he was! The object of our search, the dread Caliph Oneiroi, the Sender of Dreams. We were utterly unprepared, having been drawn to this very room at the heart of his strength, at his very bidding. As we entered, he looked up at us with grey, forbidding eyes and uttered a single word; a final pronouncement of doom upon the remainder of our lives. The pages of the book fluttered and from them arose a squamous misshapen form which defied all description. It oozed and slithered toward us and we readied what weapons we had; knives of steel with which we tried to penetrate its thick, rubbery hide to no avail. Whatever this loathsome abomination was, we could not even injure it and were forced to retreat in haste as waves of blistering insanity finally overtook us.

The last thing I recall was a hasty rush to the door - a last, desperate hope of escape. I must find the passage back to our own reality! To the normalcy of the desert heat, the call of the muezzins in that now far-off city where we had started this foolish escapade! As we ran pell-mell from the umbral tentacles, through room after identical room, we knew we were doomed. Numbness overcame us, a desire to remain here in perpetuity, to relax and give in to the worst excesses of our minds and become as one with the horror of the uncaring, inhospitable universe and its dark, terrible secrets. It seemed we could never leave now, but with one last great surge of will, we finally managed to triumph. When we turned around, the palace was no more.

Carnival In The Woods

Diane Arrelle

Kenny followed the narrow, rutted, dirt road into the forest without much thought. He had laughed when the local hicks out here called him names, including the oldest, lamest name of all, "chicken." He wasn't afraid, he wasn't afraid of anything except dying too soon, but following a muddy road called the Ghost Path certainly wasn't on his list of "scary."

"Sure, no problem," he'd said to the five teenagers who had gotten off their ATVs as soon as they saw him walking across a dead cornfield. He knew they were thinking, "fresh victim to scare." But he wasn't anyone's victim, except cancer.

"Yo," one yelled. "You new around here?"

Kenny sighed. He hated teenagers even though he was one. Especially ones that formed a gang around him. "Nope, just visiting for the weekend." *Yeah,* he thought with a bitter taste, *the weekend.* Mom and Dad were convinced a visit to the country was just the ticket to improve his health. *They have to know I'm going to die with or without fresh air.*

He listened to the hicks weave their tales of ghosts and unspeakable horrors, each trying to be scarier than the other. Finally, he asked, "Have any of you ever lost anyone to the Ghost Path?"

One spoke up, "Well, no, but a friend of my grandfather's said his uncle went in and never came out."

Kenny snorted. "A friend of your grandfather? Seriously? Ok, have any of you gone in the woods along the path?"

"No, we're not stupid. You go in, you die."

Kenny snorted again, *Not stupid, huh*? "Well, it seems pretty stupid to believe tales like that."

He smirked, the gauntlet was thrown down.

Another of them said, "Yeah, you think you're so smart, I dare you to follow the Ghost Path... all the way to the end and back."

Kenny smiled, more a sneer of disdain, "Sure, anything to get away from you guys."

He went in and was immediately hit with the aroma of leaves; fallen, crunchy leaves smelling of autumn and earthy decay.

He went deeper into the forest and the ground went from sun dappled to completely shadowed. The early afternoon took on the feel of dusk and a sharp feeling of uneasiness crept into Kenny's bones, along with the late October chill that comes when the sunshine stops. He kept moving, following the narrowing path. He watched for movement, but there was none, everything was still and silent except for his footsteps crackling the leaves.

He stopped and closed his eyes. The silence was overwhelming. It made his skin crawl. *Where were the squirrels, the bunnies, the birds*? He opened his eyes and gasped. There in front of him were gravestones. They were old; thin, worn slabs covered in moss and vines, tilting at odd angles. He knelt, running his fingers across the surface of one. He tried to read the name but time had eroded it. All that could be deciphered was the date - 1803. No other date to signify whether it was a birth or death date. He stood up, shuddered and turned around, forced to let out a yelp of fear. The path he'd been following was gone. In its place were more gravestones.

"What the heck is going on!" Kenny yelled. He turned around again and saw even more grave markers. He turned again and again until he had no idea which way he'd gotten to this place. All he knew was he had to get out. "I'm not spending my last few days before Chemo being lost in some stupid forest with a bunch of dead people for company."

He turned one more time for good measure and started walking with no idea which way he was going. No sun shadows meant he hadn't a clue where the path was. All he knew was the Ghost Path had vanished. He moved forward and the tombstones in front of him were suddenly gone.

"Huh," he grunted, surprised at all the trees facing him. He looked back and saw nothing but the trunks of more trees. No cemetery, no grave markers, just trees forming a canopy of colorful leaves above him and brush and vines around his feet. The trees were so close together, he had to suck in his breath to squeeze between them. He shuddered, fear crawling up his throat from the pit of his stomach. *Maybe*, he thought in a wave of panic that made the autumn chill even colder, *there were even worse things than Chemo.* He desperately wanted to get away from this place and pushed forward.

He heard music. Calliope music and, happy screams bubbling with laughter. The smell of decaying summer replaced with the smell of popcorn, peanuts, candy apples and apple cider.

Kenny stopped walking for a second, then smiled. *See, nothing to be afraid of after all,* he thought and rushed through the crowded forest toward what had to be a carnival. "Some endless forest!" he said as he shed his fear and laughed. "Boy, were those hicks really dumb."

The trees thinned and then vanished, just like the cemetery did, but he didn't care. There it was. Rides, refreshment stands, games of chance, a banner reading 'All Hallows Eve Fair.'

He looked around and, like the cemetery, the woods he'd just come through were nowhere in sight. He found himself standing in the middle of the fair. Discomfort gnawed at him, but he decided he had no other choice; no matter which way he went he was in the midway. A clown, a happy faced clown, stopped and looked him over. The clown's face took on a sad look and his painted, bright red smile somehow turned into a frown. He gently laid his hand on Kenny's head and then moved down to touch Kenny's chest. A make-up tear formed at the clown's eye and rolled down his cheek like a computer graphic. Then his painted smile returned and he handed Kenny a bright blue balloon.

It was the creepiest thing Kenny had ever seen. How could a face covered in make-up change like that? It looked like something out of a horror movie. He looked at the balloon he was holding and swore he could still feel the clown's soft touch, right where his cancer had returned.

He tried to forget about dying for a while. He was given a soda and a box of popcorn by other people at the fair. No one spoke but they smiled and handed him stuff. He walked up to the Ferris wheel and saw an empty car waiting for him. He got in and an old man appeared and closed the car door.

The ride began. The wheel was huge, reaching way above the trees. The wheel turned until he was at the top where he looked all around and could see no end to the forest. It seemed to go on forever in every direction. He wasn't cold any more, in fact the air felt warm like a perfect June night. He shrugged out of his lightweight jacket and noticed that the sun was just about to set. The sky was streaked with gold and pink, making the colorful tree tops glow in the warm light.

It was beautiful. Probably the most beautiful thing he'd ever seen. He felt a lump in his throat and tears on his cheeks as he realized that this was very likely the last breathtaking sunset he'd ever live to see. Monday he was going back to the hospital. All the tests had already been done and he knew this chemo treatment was a last ditch effort, too little too late.

He'd had his last remission. The doctors had talked to him, but his parents couldn't give up. After all, they were his mother and father. He was their child and if they held onto every last strand of hope, maybe they could be right. He knew deep inside that the end was near, but he kept that last bit of hope inside him too. Just in case miracles were real.

The ride ended. "I should go back," he said aloud. He didn't want to leave, ever, but his parents would be worried. Nothing happened. The carnival remained as it was, surrounded by walls of night darkened forest.

He shrugged, realized that he had no idea for how to get home and thought, *well maybe one more ride*. He went to the spinning cups, twirling round and round as the base they sat on rotated around in a wider circle. The ride stopped and children got off. They laughed and smiled but they did not talk to him.

"So weird," he muttered, and took a cup to sit in. The ride began and he laughed, feeling like a carefree kid. He loved the tight feeling in his stomach as he spun round and round. He liked feeling dizzy from a ride rather than dizzy from treatments. "I wish, I could stay here!" he shouted and the ride screeched to a halt. *What happened?* he wondered. *Why'd it stop?*

A boy walked up to his cup and got on. The ride started up but slowly. "Do you really like it here?" the boy asked. "Would you stay?"

Kenny blinked. "It's fun, but I gotta get home."

"If you go home, you won't survive. If you go home, the carnival will not be here for you. Ever again."

Kenny felt the ride gaining speed, "I don't understand what you're talking about. I don't even understand why there's a carnival in the middle of a forest and no one knows about it."

They whipped round and round and Kenny was surprised he could hear the boy perfectly.

"This is a place for people to be happy. They were not able to be happy in life. The carnival is their home now."

Kenny thought a moment, "In life? You mean everyone here is dead?"

The boy shook his head no. "Many are, many are chosen to join early. Like you. The doomed ones."

"Are you a ghost?"

The boy smiled and nodded yes.

"What is this place?"

"A carnival, that's all, just not one anchored to earthly restraints."

"Who's in charge?"

The boy shrugged. "I guess the Ghost Path is. It decides who gets out of the forest, who stays lost in the cemetery… and who is welcome here."

Kenny went still. "How long would I stay here?"

"That's your choice. The carnival is here every All Hallows Eve. Those that want to leave, the path is open to them, but it is always a one-way path."

"I'd like to stay, I really would, but what about my parents?"

"You may see them again, that's your choice when to leave. If you go now, you'll see your mother and father, but not for long."

199

Kenny didn't want to, but he knew what the boy meant. He knew it would be horrible for his parents if he disappeared into the woods. They'd be heartbroken and there'd be no closure for them, only questions and pain. He also knew he would die if he left here. "Medical science is improving every year. Why, I bet they'll have a cure in a year or two. I can leave here then. Mom and Dad will be thrilled when I come back and can be healthy."

The boy nodded. "Yes, that could happen."

Kenny knew his choice was selfish, even heartless, but he didn't want to die in a hospital when this place was giving him a chance. He pushed the guilt far back into his subconscious and said, "Well, then, I think I'll stay awhile."

People suddenly smiled and waved to him. The boy said, "Welcome to our family, but be warned, you better eat everything you like before midnight and be sure to pick your favorite ride, because at the witching hour the carnival leaves this forest and whatever you're doing, you'll be doing until the carnival returns here."

"A whole year?"

"Well, not exactly a year. It goes much quicker than real time here and the alive ones of us never seem to grow or change." The boy smiled at Kenny. Then he quickly added, "I suggest not doing a spinning ride right now. It's hard to twirl continuously for a long time. You have to build up to it."

Kenny smiled back, feeling really alive for the first time in an age, "You have a name?"

"Charlie."

"Well, Charlie, I'm Kenny. Why don't we go eat ourselves silly? Then what do you say to a year's worth of the roller coaster?"

The Monsters In Your Head

Wendy Lynn Newton

Tired?
Anxious?
Overthinking and unable to sleep?
Let Themon Stersin Yourhead Inc. and our patented
ReleasetheBeast™ technology release your demons
and give you a new lease on life.
Imagine becoming the person you were always
meant to be.

I crumpled the flyer into a ball and was aiming it at the bin when the words *what do you have to lose* hit my eyeline. I slumped and rubbed a hand over my eyes. I was tired, anxious, unable to sleep. Definitely overthinking. But who wasn't these days? It was 2037 after all; you couldn't get to 42 and survive years of pandemics, financial crashes and relationship breakdowns without cracking a few eggs or, in my case - and those of my friends - a few minds.

Imagine becoming the person you were always meant to be.

I flattened the ball onto the kitchen benchtop, smoothing the paper and releasing the creases.

Our gentle, but effective program with its patented technology sweeps those unwanted thoughts, disquieting anxieties and brutal nightmares from your mind, so you can get on with your life - and all over one tiny lunch break.

I couldn't remember the last time I had a lunch break, even a tiny one, but most days felt like a nightmare, especially with the staff I had. Being a small business owner was hard enough without the crap that went along with employing people and these days I was starting to feel more like the mouse running on the wheel than the one who feeds the cheese. It seemed the whole world had gone mad, and that madness was there when you got to work in the morning, it was there on the train ride home in the afternoon, it was there when you turned the news on in the evening, it was there in the alcoholic haze when you stumbled into bed.

"You're too nice, that's the problem," Sherie kept telling me. "You let people take advantage of you. Start being as awful as the rest of us, then you'll get ahead, it's the simple law of nature. Kill or be killed."

She kept repeating that right up until the day she left me and cleaned out all the bank accounts. Then she kept telling me in the constant, nagging voice that didn't leave me when she did. Put that to the growing list of troubles I was trying not to deal with and it added up to my own homegrown psychopath in my head.

Too nice. I didn't feel nice.

Bitter and twisted was more like it.

I turned the paper over.

Call 1800-ReleasetheBeast and enjoy our 10% introductory discount - and set your demons free!

Before I knew it, I had made an appointment with Themon Stersin Yourhead Inc. and was sitting in their packed waiting room. Their offices took up one floor of an opulent, historic building in the city fringes, the sort that is full of marble floors and stone archways that seem to go on forever. It reeked of success and I was starting to relax as I admired the row of antique lanterns lining either side of the long hallway, when I heard someone say, "Albert Starling?"

A tall, slender man dressed entirely in black approached my raised hand and held out a bony one in response. "I'm Mr Themon of Themon Stersin Yourhead Incorporated, I'll be your co-pilot today, Mr Starling, your partner-in-crime for the first day of the rest of your life."

He offered a thin-lipped smile after his hand and I returned a weak one back. Mr Themon looked more like an undertaker than a co-pilot for the rest of my life, even with the cheesy line, but maybe that was a sign he'd be burying my psychoses today.

I could only hope.

"Let's get you signed up and get started, I'm sure you're a busy man."

"Before we do that," I said, scrambling to keep up with him as he made his way to a broad reception desk strangely bare of a receptionist and everything else, "how does all this work?"

"I'm afraid our technology is patented, Mr Starling, I'm unable to -"

"Just broadly speaking," I said.

He took a sharp breath in and glanced at his watch and I could see the tedium gather in the narrowing of his eyes.

"It's quite simple really," he said, pulling out some papers from behind the desk. "We download your worrying thoughts using our unique ReleasetheBeast™ technology and upload them to the cloud, where they're out in the ether, instead of piling up inside your head."

He eased a rather long application form over the leather blotter towards me - curiously, I noticed that all my personal information had already been filled in - and my gaze slid over the rather long disclaimer partially obscured by his hand and the finger tapping at the words *Payment in Advance.*

"All it takes is one flourish of your pen and you can simply -" he gestured theatrically, "let them free."

"But if everyone's demons are released into the cloud -" I stopped, glancing back towards the crowded waiting room, "won't they… accumulate?"

"Imagine an oil spill in a vast ocean," he said. "The oil gushes at the point where the pipe breaks, but then the waves disperse it like fog on a wind. Eventually, you would never ever know it was ever even there."

"But oil kills a lot of fish before it's dispersed," I said.

"It's just an analogy, Mr Starling," he replied, waving two fingers at me in dismissal. "You

205

mustn't take it so literally. I can assure you the procedure is very safe. For everyone."

He sniffed and I could see from the terse line of his mouth that he wasn't impressed with my somewhat argumentative statement.

"Your head is the pipe, Mr Starling, from what you've told me, I fear, ready to burst. Let us help ease that rancid oil from your mind. Let us help you to -" he blew a fictitious feather from the tips of his fingers, "let it go."

Desperation and the constant tapping of Mr Themon's finger on the desk as I tried to read the disclaimer, saw me sign the release form without fully understanding what I was really disclaiming, apart from clearing Themon Stersin Yourhead Inc. from all liability - including any bad effects, undesirable impacts, unforeseeable events and calamitous catastrophes in all future generations of Starlings. Despite his assurances that the procedure was very safe.

For everyone.

Before I had time to reconsider, he snatched the paper and pen from my hand, and thrust them both under the counter.

"If you'd like to come this way," he said.

I followed him into a dimly lit corridor, with only the old lanterns flickering as if with candlelight and then into a room that lit up with such startling white-light intensity I felt myself blinded and blinking uncontrollably.

"Please, take a seat," he said, indicating a chair - the only chair - a smartly covered wingback covered in a snake of cables, leads, switches and

206

plugs. "Ms Stersin will be with you shortly." He was at the door when he turned back and said, "Try to relax, Mr Starling, it's much easier to let them go when you do."

It was only a lone moment before Ms Stersin swept into the room, all white-coated, impersonal precision, with a curt nod of her head and a somewhat formal, "Mr Starling, if you're ready to begin."

I felt my throat thicken as she punched some data into a nearby monitor.

"Will I feel anything?" I asked as she placed the first cup on top of my head. I felt the tug on my hair as she readjusted it and roughly followed the cup with three more, as if my hair was answering the question.

"Not at first," she replied, continuing to straighten out cables and plugging different USBs into various ports.

"But after that?" I asked.

"We can't be responsible for any bad effects, undesirable impacts, unforeseeable events and calamitous catastrophes," she said without taking her eyes off the monitor. "You did sign the waiver?"

Before I could answer, or ask anything else, she asked, "Ready?" as her red-polished finger hovered over a small, green switch with the word Release written above it.

I'm not sure I said yes. I'm not sure about much of anything until I woke up in the recovery room and realised the procedure was over. I tried to sit up,

207

but only got part way before falling back onto the bed, my head throbbing like I'd been hit about a dozen times with Thor's hammer.

"Mr Starling!" I heard Mr Themon shout from the doorway. "Please do not disrupt the healing process by moving, you must stay still until we have discharged you." He sighed and pranced over to the end of the bed, picked up my chart and ran a finger over my data. "I really wish you'd paid attention to the consent form, it's very clearly spelled out. We can't be responsible for any bad effects, undesirable impacts -"

"It's done?" I asked.

Mr Themon smiled. "Well and truly. All gone, every last one of them, there will be no monsters in your head, guaranteed. You'll be able to go home and start your new life, just as soon as I -"

His eyes narrowed and I saw his finger stop at a particular point on my chart.

"Well, this is odd," he muttered, "I wonder if Ms Stersin has seen this." Mr Themon glanced over his shoulder and I saw his face redden when he turned back.

"Something's odd?" I asked, feeling my heart jerk as I tried to sit up again.

"Just a little anomaly, a rather strong attachment, it seems, nothing to worry about, I'm sure. It's all gone now." He gave me a big smile and the chart a big tick with a flourish of his red pen. "There, all done. Would you like to see them?"

"See them?" I repeated as he helped my legs over the side of the bed.

"Yes, I can take you to the viewing room. Not everyone does, it's really up to you, some people like to say goodbye."

I followed him down the corridor, still groggy from the after-effects of whatever had just happened, until we stopped in front of a large, mirrored window.

"Ready?" Mr Themon asked cheerily and before I could nod, he flicked a switch on the wall and the mirrored surface disappeared.

"My, my, Mr Starling, no wonder you've had trouble sleeping."

A thick black smoke was swirling within a small, tiled room and various coloured lights pulsed within the dark cloud of it, as if technicolour lightning was flashing in a brooding storm. Through the glass I could hear muffled sounds, cries, maniacal laughter, angry shouts and swearing, I even imagined I could hear Sherie's nagging voice telling me I was way too nice and would never make anything of myself. I felt my stomach roll and gripped the edge of the window as a wave of dizziness passed over me.

"Please don't tap the glass!" Mr Themon growled, "you don't want to raise their attention."

But it was too late. I saw a distinct shape start to emerge from the blackness, somewhat human in form, but much larger than any man I'd ever seen, with a grotesque, bulbous hump on its back that made it lean over to one side. When it's cold, yellow eyes fixed on me through the black fog I found myself turning nervously away.

"There, there, Mr Starling, they'll start to disappear shortly, they can't live without an attachment. Say goodbye to the monsters in your head," and with that Mr Themon flicked a small, green switch with the word Release written above it.

I was bundled towards and out the back door before I could ask what side effects, if any, I might experience, despite Mr Themon's cheery suggestion I should call if I experienced any.

"What number?" I asked, but the slamming of the door behind me was the only response I got and the very last time I heard from Mr Themon.

I made my way to my car, a little unsteady on my feet. I had no idea how long I'd been in recovery, but the day had turned into night and the night had turned cold - so much for it supposedly taking place over one tiny lunch break. I sat for a moment revving the engine, rubbing my hands together as I waited for the heater to come on, wondering what other truths they might have embellished - or left out entirely - when I felt, more than saw, a shadow appear behind me in the back seat. The shadow was followed by a pair of cold, yellow eyes gazing across my shoulder into the rearview mirror.

"Hello, Albert," the psychopath that was now out of my head said. "I hear from Sherie that you're way too nice and it's holding you back in life. Tutt-tutt, we can soon fix that. Shall we have a nice chat when we get home?"

Meet the Authors

Dan Allen is Canadian and enjoys spending time in Northern Ontario. You can find his short stories in numerous magazines, anthologies and podcasts. Visit www.danallenhorror.com to see a presentation of his published work.

His terrifying look at Alzheimer's, "Above the Ceiling," is featured in Bards and Sages collection of the Best Indie Speculative Fiction Vol. 2.

A personal favourite, "Sympathy for the Zingara," can be found in the March 2019 edition of ParAbnormal Magazine.

His terrifying story, "The Basement" (edited by Horror Zine's Jeani Rector), was published by Hellbound Books in July 2020.

You can visit Dan at www.danallenhorror.com and follow him on Facebook and Twitter at @danallenhorror. You can write to Dan at contact@danallenhorror.com

Olivia Arieti lives in Torre del Lago Puccini, Italy, with her family. She writes drama, poetry and fiction. Her stories have appeared in several magazines and anthologies including, *Enchanted Conversations, Enchanted Tales Literary Magazine, Fantasia Divinity Magazine, Forgotten Tomb Press, Horrified Press, Infective Ink, Pandemonium Press, Sirens Call Publications, Blood Song Books, Black Hare Press, Pussy Magic Magazine, Stormy Island Publishing, Breaking Rules Publishing, Scarlet Leaf Review, Iron Faerie Publishing, Dark Dossier*

Magazine, Paramour Ink Press, Raven and Drake Publishing

Dorothy Davies is an editor, writer, photographer and medium. Somehow all these things come together in her seemingly crowded leisure and work life. She is an avid kindle user and delights in writing reviews for Amazon, especially when a novel is deleted a mere 2-3 chapters in and is too badly written to be read... she retired from editing for a while to run a second hand shop, the best one on the Isle of Wight, but the thrill of finding and publishing outstanding stories became too much so she started again with the Gravestone Press imprint. She still runs the shop...

Joseph Dowling has pursued many interests and diverse career paths, always knowing he would write seriously one day.

In 2020, now owner of a small but previously thriving chain of retro arcade bars temporarily shuttered due to Covid-19, he fell into an obsession.

Since finding the passion, Joseph can't imagine life without the stories constantly rattling around his head. Eager to make up for lost time; he's in the habit of writing every day, becoming a keen student of the craft. He recently had his first acceptance and will appear in an upcoming anthology called 'Worlds Collide'.

Arlen Feldman As well as writing fiction, Arlen is a software engineer, entrepreneur, maker, and computer book author—useful if you are in the market for some industrial-strength door stops. Some recent stories of his appear in the anthologies *The Chorochronos Archives* and *Particular Passages,* and in *On The Premises* magazine, with several more coming out soon. His website is cowthulu.com.

Jason R Frei lives in Eastern Pennsylvania where he works as a therapist with children and adolescents. He writes speculative fiction culled from the experiences of his life and those he works with and blends science fiction, fantasy and horror into new creations. His flash story "The Garden" will be featured in the horror anthology *99 Tiny Terrors* by Pulse Publishing and his short story "Some of the Parts" will be featured in the horror anthology *Toilet Zone 3: The Royal Flush* by Hellbound Books Publishing. Visit him online: https://facebook.com/odinstones.

Ken L Jones, story teller and poet extraordinary is no longer with us but there are still collections of startling and beautiful poems for us to appreciate.

Chris Marchant lives abroad with her partner and far too many cats. She writes mainly science fiction, fantasy and historical, but veers off course now and then. She is currently working on an historical Gamelit/LitRPG novel.

Her website is www.chrismarchantwriter.com. She also has guardianship of #Drizztthemusecat.

Rickey Rivers Jr was born and raised in Alabama. He is a Best of the Net nominated writer and cancer survivor. His work has appeared in the JJ Outre Review, Stellium Literary Magazine, Fabula Argentea (among other publications).

Rie Sheridan Rose multitasks. A lot. Her short stories appear in numerous anthologies, including Killing It Softly Vol. 1 & 2, Hides the Dark Tower, Dark Divinations and On Fire. She has authored twelve novels, six poetry chapbooks and lyrics for dozens of songs. She is also editor-in-chief for Mocha Memoirs Press and editor for the Thirteen O' Clock imprint of Horrified Press. She tweets as @RieSheridanRose.

Liam A Spinage is a former philosophy student, former archaeology educator and former police clerk who spends most of his spare time on the beach gazing up at the sky and across the sea while his imagination runs riot.

SJ Townend hopes that her stories take the reader on a journey to often a dark place and only sometimes back again. SJ won the Secret Attic short story contest (Spring 2020), has had fiction published with Sledgehammer Lit Mag, Hash Journal, Ghost Orchid Press, Bandit Fiction, Black Hare Press, Black Petals Horror Magazine, Ellipsis Zine, Gravely Unusual, Gravestone Press, Holy Flea, Horla Horror and was long listed for the Women on Writing non-fiction contest in 2020. She has also written and self-published two dark mystery novels, both of which are available to purchase on Amazon: (Tabitha Fox Never Knocks, Twenty-Seven and the Unkindness of Crows). Follow her on Twitter: @SJTownend

David Turnbull is a member of the Clockhouse London group of genre writers. He writes mainly short fiction and has had numerous short stories published in magazines and anthologies. His stories have previously been featured at Liars League London events and read at other live events such as Solstice Shorts and Virtual Futures. He was born in Scotland, but now lives in the Catford area of London. He can be found at **www.tumsh.co.uk.**

Diane Arrelle has more than 350 short stories published and two short story collections: Just A Drop In The Cup and Seasons On The Dark Side. She, her sane husband and insane cat live on the edge of the New Jersey (USA) Pine Barrens (home of the Jersey Devil).

www.arrellewrites.com   FaceBook: Diane Arrelle

Wendy Lynn Newton is an Australian fiction and non-fiction writer. She is the author of two non-fiction books and her short stories and feature articles have appeared in many key international and Australian literary and media publications. Wendy is a Full Member of the Australian Society of Authors and spent several years as a member of Write Response, a team of independent Tasmanian arts reviewers, after being selected by Arts

Tasmania for an arts@work mentorship. She is currently working on a young adult science fiction trilogy and lives in northern Tasmania with two out-of-control Chihuahuas and two indifferent cats.

wendy.newton.launceston@gmail.com
Instagram: @wendynewtonlaunceston

Lightning Source UK Ltd.
Milton Keynes UK
UKHW041002110722
405676UK00001B/20

9 781786 957856